SIEBOLD

A BERSERKER WARRIOR ROMANCE

LEE SAVINO

SILVERWOOD PRESS, LLC

CONTENTS

FREE BOOK

SIEBOLD

A wounded warrior wants to claim me as mate...

For years I've lived alone in the deep woods, hiding my powers from the world. But when I meet a wounded wolf on a forest path, I can't bear his suffering. I call on my magic to heal him.

Then he follows me home and I find he's no ordinary wolf. He's a Berserker warrior, cursed long ago to become a ravening monster. His only hope: find the woman who can tame his beast.

Siebold thinks that woman is me.

But this handsome warrior doesn't just want me to lift the curse. Siebold wants me. All of me. And he'll possess me: body, soul, and heart.

Because nothing can stop a Berserker when he decides you're his mate.

Siebold is a standalone warrior romance set in the Berserker world. You don't need to read the rest of the Berserker books to enjoy this one, but Berserkers are like a box of chocolates: best devoured in entirety in one sitting...

M eadhan

I WAS HALFWAY to the market when I sensed I was being followed.

No twigs snapped. No birds sang. No insects droned. But the silence spoke louder than any sound.

Somewhere, in the secret shadows of the forest, lurked a predator.

Prickles danced up and down my limbs. I turned slowly in place, one arm tight around my herb-filled basket, the other cupping the back of my neck where my skin tingled.

Something was watching me. I stared into the sun-dappled shadows, willing them to reveal their secrets.

I did not know what I was looking for. Most forest predators respected me. Or the power they sensed in me. But not this one. I peered into the underbrush. What animal would be so hungry and desperate to venture this close to the village?

I should have kept on my way, hurrying to the safety of the crowded market, but something stayed my steps. An awareness, a pressure on the edge of my consciousness.

It wasn't just an animal stalking me. I sensed something Other. A darkness buzzing like an angry swarm of bees.

Evil.

Magic.

"Who's there?" I called, unable to help myself. I didn't expect an answer.

Deep in the brush, the branches parted. The whining sound and pressure on my ears and skin increased. My hand flew out, sketching a ward before I knew what I was doing. It was a basic sign of protection, one my mother taught me before I could walk. As soon as I signed it, I snatched my hand back, and gripped my basket so hard my knuckles whitened.

I never practiced my craft this close to the village. But whatever lurked in the brush made me want to call my power.

My vision shimmered, my Sight taking hold. There in the shadows under the pine, stood a big blond warrior. His arms and chest were bare but thatched with white weals of old scars. His face bore a thick blond beard. But his eyes were haggard. He was a warrior who'd seen many battles and survived the slaughter and now he was old and tired. Older than he looked, for he seemed the same age as me, yet there was a century of pain in his golden eyes.

"Who are you? What do you want?" I whispered, though I knew the vision was not real. I stepped back anyway, sucking in a breath when the man disappeared, his form winking out of existence as if he was a ghost.

The bushes before me rustled, and a wolf emerged. He was big and blond--his fur the same shade as the hair of the warrior in my vision. But that color is natural among wolves. There was nothing to mark this wolf as anything unnatural.

Then it turned its head and caught me in its golden gaze. Its eyes blazed with eldritch light. Just as the warrior's had.

This was no ordinary wolf.

"What happened to you?" I whispered.

The wolf lurched forward with half whine, half growl and pushed out of its hiding place. Its body was long and lean, but too thin. Ribs showed through its matted fur. Its mouth hung open, flashing yellowed fangs thicker than my fingers.

An ordinary woman would run and hope she reached the village before she was attacked and brought down by those teeth and claws. Good sense would say this was a wild creature, a wolf mad enough with hunger to venture close to the village where a hunter's arrow would put it out of misery. For a crazed wolf, death would be a mercy.

But this was not just a wolf. My Sight had never guided me wrong.

I crouched on the path, averting my gaze and inclining my head so it was lower than the wolf's. A submissive posture.

The wolf padded forward. Its head twitched sharply, as if shaking flies from around its ears. As it came close the buzzing of evil magic filled my ears. The stench of rot hung over its body.

"Bad magic," I breathed. My mother told me of a special breed of warriors, cursed by a witch to take the form of wolves. The spell was meant to give them power. But, like all spells, it came with a price. "You wretched beast." I reached for my herbs and the wolf let out a growl. I froze at the low rumbling sound.

"Stop that," I snapped. I may have taken a submissive posture, but I would not tolerate rudeness. Not even from a wolf.

The wolf blinked at me, and stopped its growl. With swift fingers, I twisted together rosemary, cedar, juniper, and sage. Herbs for memory, clarity, and purification.

"This won't break the spell, but it will help." I tossed the bundle at the wolf's feet. Its only reaction was to lower its head and sniff, then sneeze. I stifled a smile. This wolf was dangerous, even if it was acting tame. It snuffed, its nose twitching once, twice. The jerky movement of its head calmed. It raised its head again and I Saw the evil hovering over it, manifesting as a dark swarm of flies.

I jerked up my hands and called my power.

The magic within me uncoiled slowly, moving through my limbs with a golden ripple. First only a trickle, then a steady stream, as if I'd unstopped a dam. The power wanted to flow from me in a wide arc, a flood.

The clean swath of magic met the buzzing evil of the wolf's curse, and swept it away.

The wolf turned and ran. My power chased it, rolling over its giant furred body, searching for evil magic so it could wash it clean.

I tried to stop the flow of power, snatch it back, but it was too strong. A wild beast, longing to rage untamed.

It'd been too long since I'd allowed myself to use my powers. Even now, the golden current flowed through me, imbuing my limbs with power. The pressure rose behind my eyes as I tried to stuff it back into its cage. My stomach lurched and I staggered when it was done, feeling as if I'd bottled a raging river.

One day I would not be able to stem the tide. I would wield my power in front of everyone, and they all would know what I was.

But not today. I gathered up my basket and prepared to hurry down the well-trodden path as if I was an ordinary woman on her way to market. Before I turned away, a wind lifted the hairs at the back of my neck. I heard a whisper in the breeze, but I couldn't make out the words.

I looked again for the golden wolf, but it was gone.

2

S *iebold*

THE FLIES BUZZED around my head. I snapped at them and they disappeared into dust motes dancing in the sun. The flies weren't real. But still the buzzing whined inside my head. I scratched and scratched until the scent of blood rose in the air. Thorns stabbed me--I'd shredded my ears with my claws. The magic of the curse healed my ears in a sick-making surge. I gagged, tongue lolling in the air.

And that's how I caught the scent. Sweet and light, sun rays and honey sizzling on my tongue. The angry buzzing dimmed.

I dragged myself towards the scent, wriggling like a worm past thick hemlock branches. Twigs dug into my sides as I pushed forward.

A light appeared on the path. Bright gold. The sun come down to earth.

I pushed closer and the light coalesced into a form. A woman. Her face was haloed, her dark skin shining like the honeyed sap from a tree. Her scent billowed over me in soft waves. I lifted my nose to the clean smell. My head cleared.

The woman knelt on the path. She moved suddenly and I growled.

"Stop that," she snapped, and to my surprise, I did. It had been a long time since anyone gave me an order.

A bundle of green landed at my feet. I sniffed and sneezed at the harsh herbal scent. She murmured something again, words I could almost understand, if the flies buzzing around my head hadn't started again. My flesh crawled, the evil within surging to attack.

If I had any honor, I'd run until I found a sea to drown in, and save this woman made of light. But the curse had me in its grip.

And then the sun before me blazed and drove every bit of madness from my bones. The immense power clamped down and shook me in its grip. I scrambled backwards, and it chased me, tingling up my back and ruffling my fur. I raced until I was out of its reach. But it was too late.

When it was gone, so were the flies. The buzzing and the rotten stench had been washed off my fur. The madness I'd worn like a decrepit cloak had burned away. Nothing stood between me and my memories.

Once I was a man. I stood on two feet. I held an axe in my hand.

And I destroyed every good thing. I broke the bonds of honor and was cast out by my pack. They banished me to the magic that would eat me alive. They gave me to the madness, the mind rot that was both punishment and my only companion.

That time was long gone. But now, because of her, I remembered.

I shut my eyes and willed the buzzing madness to return.

3

M eadhan

THE MARKET STARTED on the edge of the village and covered a large field. My stall was right along the forest edge, where few liked to tread. It suited me just fine. My customers preferred privacy when they sought me.

They darted between the animal pens and hustled my way, heads down and gaze sweeping left and right. Only when they're sure no one they knew was watching did they scuttle forward, ducking into the frame I'd covered in woven branches to make a covered tent.

"Mistress?" A man with graying hairs and a meek expression appeared beside my stall. He glanced this way and that before leaning close to whisper, "Last week you gave my wife some herbs. They were black, like mushrooms. They helped with... a problem she had."

I suppressed my smile and rooted out the herbs in question, a bundle of black ginger, native to lands far east where I lived in my youth. They do not like the soil here, but my power bids them to push through the soil each year.

I murmured the price. The older man handed over the fee without protest. I did smile at his back when he walked away. His wife was a lucky woman.

As the sun climbed higher, more villagers dared walk by me. Two girls lingered at my table, giggling and whispering to each other while I portioned herbs for a heavily pregnant woman. When my pregnant customer toddled off, I turned to the girls. I recognized them.

"Alys and Eira, greetings."

"Hello, Mistress." The girls blushed when I called them by name. One unlinked her arm from her friend and picked up a bottle of infused honey.

"Is it true this will make a boy love me?"

I smiled. The girls were no longer giggling.

"There is no such thing as a love potion," I lied. "But there are many ways to a man's heart."

Their eyes grew wider in their faces as they leaned further in. I heard the jingle of the coins in their pockets. Coins that would soon be in my hand.

"Make a man honey cakes and he might find reason to woo you," I told them.

Alys pushed her coins towards me, her gaze fixed on the herbs.

"Alys, Eira!" A male voice snapped. "Do your mothers know where you are?"

The girls shrank before the burly, bare-pated man in priest's robes who bustled up to my stall. Under the table, I made a ward sign against evil. Ironic, considering the priest thought I was the evil.

"No, Father Gerald." The girls backed away from my stall and began to slink off.

"Wait," I grabbed the jar of honey and rounded the table to approach Alys. "You forgot your purchase."

Alys shook her head quickly and fled. Father Gerald smirked at me. "She doesn't want it."

"Here," I held the jar out to him and felt satisfaction as his eyes widened. "Take it."

"I have no need of anything you brew," he sputtered, backing away as if I'd offered him an adder. He lifted his robes and marched away, chin in air.

"It's a donation," I called after him. "For the poor."

"What's this, then?" A round, red-faced woman hustled up. Unlike the others who slunk, she did not lower her voice. "Mistress Meadhan, how kind of you to donate your goods to the needy."

"Mistress Donna," I dipped my head in greeting and she did the same. Then she looked in the direction of the retreating priest and sniffed. "Something stinks around here."

"Yes, I believe that's Father Gerald," I didn't bother to lower my voice, either. "He disapproves of bathing. Believes it's a sin."

"I'd be more tolerant of his beliefs if he kept a good distance away."

I bit back a smile.

With a final sniff, Mistress Donna briskly changed the subject. "You have the herbs for me?"

"Yes." I handed her a full basket and her cheeks grew redder and rounder in pleasure.

"Good, good. There's many women whose lives have been saved by your brews. I'll hear nothing against them."

"Thank you," I murmured. "But I have done nothing out of the ordinary."

Mistress Donna met my gaze sharply. She understood the danger of being a wise woman, a daughter of Hecate who stood in the doorway between death and life. Some people would be in awe of our gifts, but others would fear the mysteries, and condemn us.

"No of course not. We simply do our best with the bounty the earth provides. Only a fool would say otherwise." She bellowed the last part and glared at a man who was slinking past my tent, his face averted as if he did not want to greet us.

"Shame on you, Llywellyn," she scolded the man. He only scuttled away faster and she shook her head at his retreating back. "I was the first who held him at his birth. What a fool Father Gerald is."

"Fools are harmless, unless they bend the ear of a crowd, and use fear to stoke favor." I bent to rearrange my herb bundles. "Has Father Gerald been speaking against me?"

"He mistrusts any woman who does work beyond his understanding. But," she ducked her head as if examining a bunch of dried camomile. "Father Gerald is not who I'm worried about. Have you noticed the soldiers?"

"I have." I'd seen a group of them lurking on the edge of the market, heavily armed and rough looking.

"Who are they?" I asked Mistress Donna.

"Offa's men."

I schooled my features, though I knew that name.

"He wants to rule this valley. Set himself up as lord of all you can see." She flapped a hand but the worry in her tone belied her flippant act. "He's attempting to conscript men from each village to join his army."

"For what purpose?"

"To enforce his tax."

"I see," I let my cool tone give my opinion of this.

"Mmmm," Mistress Donna shook her head slightly. "Careful, Mistress Meadhan. In these dark times, a woman living alone so far from the village might not be safe."

"I will be careful," I promised. "You be sure to do the same."

"Oh, have no fear for me. I have many sons," she raised a hand and waved, and a strapping young man loped towards us. The dimpled grin stretching his red cheeks was his main resemblance to the midwife. "Alwyn," she greeted him.

"Mother," the young man gave her a kiss. "Mistress Meadhan." He turned his grin on me, and despite my disinterest in dallying with any men in this village, my stomach fluttered.

"Take these to my hearth and lay them out. Gently, now," Mistress Donna ordered, handing her son the herbs. A fond look stretched over her face as she watched Alwyn stride off. "That one gives me so much trouble," Mistress Donna said with satisfaction. "I expect he'll be the next to give me grandbabies." She turned back to me, and her smile turned sly. "Now you, Mistress Meadhan, would make a fine mother. I don't suppose you are in the market for a husband?"

I choked back a laugh at her forthright comment. "Not today. Although I hadn't realized they sold husbands at this market. I suppose it'd be a convenient way to acquire one. Like buying a goat."

"Not quite like a goat," Mistress Donna glanced back at her son and then swept her gaze over me, as if sizing me up for a wedding gown. "You just let me know if you change your mind."

"I will," I promised, though inwardly I shuddered. I had

no interest in spending my life shackled to a man, even one as handsome and genial as Mistress Donna's son seemed to be.

I did keep an eye on the rough-looking men Mistress Donna had warned me about. Offa's men. He offered protection, but if the villages would not pay him, his punishment was cruel. Offa the Bloody, they called him. He was a bullying, bragging warrior.

And his men were the same. As the sun rose high, they swaggered through the market, grabbing goods and offering little coin, and refusing to haggle. I was lucky they stayed away from my stall, though a few eyed my brown skin with curious disdain. I kept my head down and served my few customers, ignoring Father Gerald whenever he came swaggering past my stall again.

Late afternoon, my skin prickled, and I turned under the pretense of looking for some herbs in my basket. A few stalls away, Offa's men had gathered around Father Gerald. The fat priest was glancing my way and pointing. At me.

"That's the one," he said clearly, catching my eye.

No. This was how it began. Suddenly I was a child again, watching a priest point at my mother. *"Witch," he cried, and the rough men of the village came and took her and--*

No. I shut my eyes a moment. My hands were fisted at my sides. This was how it began. But I could break the cycle.

Swiftly I packed up my basket. I left a few bundles of herbs lying on the table as a gift for anyone to take. I was almost finished when someone rushed up to the stall, crying my name.

"Mistress Meadhan, come quick." It was Eira, the girl from the village. Her face flushed from running. "You must help."

I hesitated. Father Gerald and Offa's men were watching. "What is it, child?"

"There was an accident. A boy is hurt."

"Show me," I was out of my stall and hurrying behind her before I could stop myself.

Eira led me out of the market and down a forest path. I listened, but no one followed. But any relief I felt at avoiding Offa's men vanished when we came upon the site of the accident.

A few of the village youth milled around a large fallen tree. As we approached, their ranks parted to show a boy on the ground. His leg was stretched before him, and Eira gasped at the sight of the bloody wound. Among the red was a flash of white--bone.

"What happened?" I kept my voice calm.

"We were climbing on the trunk, and he fell," Eira said.

"Run back to the village, all of you," I ordered as I lowered myself down next to the boy. "Fetch his family."

A pause. "He's the priest's bastard," another child offered. "He has no family."

A quick glance told me they were right. The boy with the broken leg was thin and dirty, his hair crawling with lice. His face was gaunt with pain, but his starved and bruised body spoke of abuse and neglect. He stank as badly as the priest.

And I was going to help him. But the fewer witnesses to what I would do, the better.

"The sun is setting. your parents will be looking for you. Go. All of you. Now."

Only Eira hesitated.

"I'll take care of him," I told her, and waited until the pattering of the children's footsteps faded.

Up close the leg looked worse. The boy's jaw was

clenched white, his eyes wide as he stared at a point beyond his leg. Brave boy. Another might have fainted.

"What's your name?" I asked, to distract him.

"Dafydd," he gasped.

"Dafydd, I'm going to heal you now." I swallowed. To do this was to put my life in his hands. It was on the tip of my tongue to ask him to promise never to tell what I'd done. But he was only a boy, and alone.

I hovered my hands over his leg and called my power. A pause, as if my magic couldn't believe it was being called so soon again after this morning. Then the flow hit me in such a rush, energy crackled down my braids. Warmth pulsed from my hands. The boy cried out, his body jerking in the grip of my magic. A light flashed and it was done.

I eased myself up on shaking limbs. The boy scrambled to his feet and backed into the fallen tree, fear written on his face.

"Your leg?" I motioned to the limb. His clothing was still ripped and bloody, but the boy was standing with weight on both legs.

He blinked and looked down as if he hadn't realized he'd been healed.

I waited a moment, but the boy remained mute. Inwardly, I sighed.

"Go to Mistress Donna," I told him. "Tell her I sent you. I'll give her two whole ginger roots if she'll feed you for a week." It would be a good trade. I was the only one who could get the root to grow, but this boy looked like he needed ten meals a day to gain his proper weight. "She has sons," I muttered to myself as I turned away. "She'll have enough food."

"Are you a demon consort?" the boy called after me. I halted but did not turn. "Father Gerald says you are."

"He is mistaken." I gathered my skirts and strode back the way I came before I said something worse.

I was almost back to the market when the weight of the boy's words hit me. *Demon consort.*

What had I done? I healed a boy who might bring down death onto my head. All my hiding, careful secrecy, ruined by one boy's broken leg.

The power in me rose up to give comfort, and I pushed it back down. Distracted, my feet stumbled. I caught myself and dusted off my hands, but people noticed. I could almost hear their thoughts... *Witch woman. Her skin is dark because her mother lay with the devil...* I would have to pack my things up tonight.

"Mistress Meadhan," A young man hustled up to me. "May I help?"

"No need," I answered briskly, shouldering my basket.

"Are you sure? I'd be happy to escort you home."

I whirled to give him the sharp edge of my tongue, and my eyes caught on his winsome dimple. It was Mistress Donna's handsome son, Alwyn. There was no fear written on his face, no disdain.

Perhaps I was overreacting.

"No, thank you. I like to walk alone. And I'm sure your mother needs you."

Alwyn leaned back on his heels, looking thoughtful. "She likes you. She'd be glad to hear I was spending time with you. Besides, if she heard I let a defenseless woman go home unescorted, she'd box my ears."

I smiled at his charm despite myself. "I thank you, but I am no ordinary woman. I am not defenseless."

He nodded, but stepped closer. "Still, there are vagabonds around," he murmured, glancing towards the group of Offa's men who still lingered in the market. "I'll at least walk you through the village."

We set off, and I found myself wishing I could feel a stir of desire for this strapping and courteous young man. Like any healthy woman my age, I'd dallied with a man, but resisted all attempts to make me into a wife.

"Thank you, Alwyn," I told him firmly when we reached the edge of the village. "Please tell your mother you did your duty."

"Take care, Mistress," he touched his forehead and sauntered off. He was a good man, and would make another a good husband. But it was best for me to avoid all attachment, lest my powers became known and I had to leave this valley suddenly.

Memory struck me: my mother hiding me in the corner of our hut while angry men pounded on the door. *You must hide,* she told me. *Hide, so you might survive.*

I was so preoccupied with these thoughts I did not notice someone was following me.

4

S *iebold*

I SLUNK along the edge of the village. The angry buzzing around my head had subsided, leaving me empty. Leaving me longing for the woman who'd blazed so brightly in my life.

So I hid in the brambles and waited. I dozed, doing my best to ignore the scent of roasting meat, the irritating bray of human voices. Once I was a fierce warrior, but now I was reduced to this pathetic thing, hanging on the edges of the places of men, waiting for the glimpse of the sun.

A wind ruffled my fur. The air had grown cool, but when I raised my head a warm draft caressed my face. I was on my feet and hustling through a grove of pine before I registered the sweet scent.

It was her. The woman I'd met on the path. She was

holding her basket and talking, talking with a villager. A man.

I lunged, but at the last moment, reason held me back. I might be seen by the villagers. And I had no right to this woman.

No, howled the beast within. *She is mine.*

Then let us hunt, my reason responded. *What predators would we be, if we startled our prey?*

The beast subsided, but I could feel him crawling below my skin. Fur rippled along my limbs and back. If the woman dallied a moment longer with another, a monster would erupt from the forest and carry her away.

For that is what I was, and would only ever be. A monster. Not even she could save me. But, in her presence, I might become whole.

The villager was saying something, but he was leaving. Without hesitation, the woman turned on her heel, and strode away. Down the path, right past me.

I followed.

Her scent held accents of herbs and spices. Her braids swung around her face and her skin glowed. I'd never seen a woman like her, and yet I couldn't look straight at her. The power within lit her up like the sun.

How would I approach her? Stealthy, like a wolf? Or proudly, like a warrior?

Maybe I could carry her off. But I had no place to keep her. I'd lived in ditches, in caves, in groves near a slow running brook or another source of water. The beast allowed me no home, no rest.

I had little to offer a woman. Not even a lodge to lock her in. Perhaps I could get some rope--

An unclean scent caught my nose. Men, unwashed,

holding iron weapons. With their clanking blades, it was a wonder I hadn't heard them before.

They were following the sun. But, unlike me, they didn't sense her light. They brought darkness and they wanted her. The woman that belonged to me. But they would not catch her and keep her, as I would. My monster recognized other, lesser monsters. And these men were evil. Hovering over their heads was a miasma, the stench of their violence and lust.

They could not take her. I would not allow it.

5

M *eadhan*

A SNARL MADE ME WHIRL. A wolf stood on the path--the blond one I'd met that morn. He was back, and looked bigger than I remembered. He stood tall on the path, his growls ripping the air--but he wasn't looking to me. Beyond him was a band of warriors--Offa's men.

I clutched my basket and backed away. For a second I was a child again, hiding in my mother's hut.

The wolf growled again.

"Call off your dog," one of the men ordered me. I stiffened. I was not a child any longer.

"It's not a dog," I spoke before I thought. "It's a wolf."

A few of the men made a sign against evil.

"It's not mine," I added, but none of the men looked like they believed me.

"It's no match for us," the leader spoke again, but he

didn't sound certain. He motioned his friends forward. A few of them edged closer to the wolf, but made no move to attack first.

The wolf attack came so fast, all I saw was a blur. One moment it stood on the path, proud, golden fur glinting in the light. The next, it was gone, and the men were scattered. Several were bowled over, flailing for their weapons. One howled, clutching his arm.

I slapped a hand over my mouth.

"Hold," shouted their leader. He'd staggered upright, clutching a sword. He glanced this way and that, flashing the whites of his eyes. "It can't take us all!"

But the wolf could. And did. With a sickening crunch of bone and splashes of red, it moved through the warrior band. Men were sobbing like babies, screaming, running away. The wolf returned to the path, faced the defeated warrior band, threw back its head and roared.

An axe struck its side. A bad hit--it bounced off, but with a spray of blood. The wolf did not yelp in pain, or show any sign it noticed. It roared again and charged.

The last of the men turned white and scrambled away.

"This isn't over," the leader shouted, presumably to me. Then he yelped and fled with the rest. I was left on the path, clutching my basket, staring dumbly at the huge beast who'd menaced an entire group of armed men...and won.

The wolf swung its head towards me. And I saw its wound, the red staining its beautiful fur. My hand flung out automatically, not to stop the wolf, but to heal.

And the wolf stayed still and let me. For the third time today I called the golden power and let it roll through me, fat, lazy ripples winding down my arms like a shimmering snake. I half expected a light to stream from my fingers to touch the wolf, but instead a wind merely ruffled its fur. My magic slid over the giant creature, licking at him and liking the taste. It found bits of the curse lurking in corners, and chased the darkness away.

When I was done, I felt drained, but whole. Like I'd run up a mountain, but my legs were pleased by the exertion, and after a short rest I'd be able to run more.

"Thank you," I told the wolf, because even after healing the small wound, I was still in his debt. I did not know what Offa's men wanted with me, but it would have been nothing good.

I turned and continued down the path. If there had ever been any fear within me of the wolf, it was gone now. I didn't question why I so easily trusted the wild beast. But we'd bonded, first this morning, and again at dusk.

Dawn and dusk are times when it is easy to use great power. My mother's words came to me easily, as if she was walking beside me. *Most babies are born in the evening or in the early morn, when the veil between worlds thins. If you work a spell at these times, take care. The balance is easily broken.*

The theory of balance was one my mother discussed with me often. Nature designed the world with balance. Night and day. Shadow and light. The sun and rain. Death and life.

Too much sun makes a desert, my mother had told me. In her travels, she'd seen deserts, so she would know.

Every gift is also a curse, Meadhan. Remember that before you use magic. Power demands a price.

What would my mother say about the wolf's curse? Was I in his debt or he in mine? I'd done my best to chase off the curse hanging over the wolf, but did that bind him to me instead?

It took a few more steps before I was brave enough to

look back, but finally I did. Sure enough, the wolf was still following me.

I stopped. "Go home. Back to your den, or wherever."

The wolf sat back on its haunches to hear my orders, its tongue hanging out as it panted.

"I do not need an escort," I almost told the wolf the same thing I'd told Alwyn, but then realized it was not true. "At least, most of the time I don't. Your help was welcome, but I can defend myself. Go now. Be a wolf."

Perhaps I'd gone crazy, talking to a wolf. But this was no ordinary wolf. Unbidden, the vision I'd seen of the blond warrior that morning came back to me, and I pushed it away.

Hoisting my basket higher on my hip, I kept walking. I sensed without looking that the wolf was following. Why was some part of me pleased?

"Very well," I said, when my hut was almost in sight, and the wolf showed no signs of disappearing into the woods and leaving me alone. "You may follow me home. But you're not coming inside." Only a foolish woman would invite a wild beast into her home. Even if he were no ordinary wolf.

"Especially because you're no ordinary wolf," I muttered to myself as I pushed my door open. I set my basket down and grabbed a jug before ducking back outside.

The blond wolf sat on the edge of my garden, its head tilted as if it were studying the neat rows. I'd latched the gate behind me, but he'd simply jumped over it.

"Where does a wolf lie?" I asked as I dipped the jug in the barrel I kept to catch rainwater. "Wherever he wants. Don't touch that!" The last was to the wolf, who had put out a paw to bat at a grape vine I'd taken pains to train onto a trellis.

It lowered its paw but didn't look at all repentant. In my

garden he looked bigger than ever, a huge beast. Sitting on his haunches, his head was almost as tall as mine. One wrong move and he'd crush my peas.

I should feel uncomfortable with a strange beast in my garden, but his presence felt oddly right.

Balance, my mother whispered.

"You may stay here tonight," I announced. "If you promise to keep out the deer."

The wolf gave me a look.

"They can be quite fierce," I murmured slyly, and went to find a large bowl. When I returned with a bowlful of water, the wolf had made his bed closer to the fence. Settled in with his great head turned toward the forest, he would be a perfect sentry.

"My carrots are safe tonight." I set the bowl down close, so he could put down his head and drink. "Water. But I cannot feed you. You'll have to find meat on your own."

The wolf yawned, opening his huge mouth to show off his teeth. Then he grinned at me, smug.

"I'm sure you're a very good hunter," I said. "But you'd be better off hunting now and then finding better shelter." I pointed to the oak leaves, curling up to show their white underbellies. "It looks like rain."

THE RAIN CAME AFTER NIGHTFALL, thick sheets that pattered loudly on the oak leaves. I sat by the fire and organized my herbs, but my thoughts returned again and again to the wolf guarding my gate.

The storm wasn't so bad. A little wind, a little rain. Nothing a wolf couldn't sustain.

But this was no ordinary wolf. I'd Seen a vision of a man.

Was it an image of who the wolf had once been? Or what the wolf could still become? If he was a man cursed, what would break the spell?

My pestle scraped against the deep stone mortar, grinding the herbs within to dust. When I set it aside, my hands were aching.

"What would you do?" I whispered to my mother, but she was not here. She'd taught me well when she was with me, but I'd been so young, and her instruction had been more of a guide to grow my own intuition.

Now I was alone and my instincts were all I had. My logic told me the wolf was trouble, but my instincts said it was futile to stay away.

I peered out my door. The wolf sat on the edge of the garden, its head and ears drooping in the heavy rain.

"Outside is where a wolf belongs," I said loudly, as if to convince myself. I slammed the door and went to bed. The rain pattered on the ceiling.

My resolve was slipping. The wolf had saved me.

The wind picked up, buffeting my small hut. Its whine sounded like a wolf, low and sorrowful.

"Oh, all right," I grumbled to the ceiling. I stuck my head out long enough to shout, "Very well. Come inside!"

I waited, closing the door slightly when the wolf shook himself on my porch.

"Do not grow accustomed to this," I muttered as it trotted past me. "I must be mad, inviting you in, talking to you like you understand."

The wolf met my gaze in a way that told me he did understand. I pushed past his giant bulk--his size made the hut smaller by half--to stoke up the fire. A creaking sound made me turn. The wolf had settled on my bed.

"No. Absolutely not." I made my voice sharp, my hands on my hips. "Down." I pointed to the floor.

The wolf bared its teeth, slowly enough I didn't find it a threat.

"Is this how you repay my kindness?"

With a huff, the wolf slunk off my bed. We eased past each other, trading places--the wolf at the hearth, me by my bed.

"That's better." I sat down on my now slightly dampened quilts.

After washing up with water from the basin, I took the time to braid my plaits. My boisterous curls would only behave in the morning if I tamped them down each night. The wolf's eyes were on me as I wove the crown around my head.

There was so much intelligence in those eyes. Its gaze was alert, curious. Its nose lifted in the air as though it wished to get closer and scent my motions. When I was done I turned from it. I pulled the quilts tightly around me. When I closed my eyes, I fell into a dream.

Angry voices and weapons clinked outside our hut. I peered through the cracks at the assembled men. They were all men from a nearby village, but the light from their torches flickered over their dirty faces, twisting their features so they looked like laughing demons.

"Meadhan--run. Hide." My mother pressed a packet of dried meat and herbs into my hands, and bundled me into a cloak. She removed a loose board at the back of our hut and pushed me out. I scrabbled on the ground, splinters in my hair, but did not run.

"Mama," I turned and reached for her, but she had withdrawn. She would not follow, would not escape with me.

Her face, white and strained, her eyes huge in her face as she snarled at me. "Go! Hide."

And I watched helpless as she went to the door and opened it, and faced the firelit mob.

"Mama! No!"

Something nudged me. A weight, thick and heavy. I stopped thrashing at the nightmare and slipped into an entirely different dream.

A man standing between the trees in the dappled light of the forest. He wears a blond wolf pelt over his shoulders. His golden skin and hair blaze brighter than the sun. I should leave, I should run, but instead I move closer, my footsteps matching the beat of my heart. He raises his head and meets my gaze and liquid honey pours over my skin. I am naked. His hands reach for me--

In the deep warmth of my bed, a rough hand traced up my thigh. Instead of pressing my knees together, I let them go lax and fall apart.

Fingers whispered over my breasts and my nipples beaded into tight points. My breath hitched. My dreams had never taken this turn, but I was thankful for the new direction. Even more, I was curious to see where it would go.

The hands traced down my belly. They parted my thighs and found the tight bud there. The pressure built like my power. I tried to contain it but I could not. Warm and golden, it poured out of me.

I was trembling when I woke up, gasping for air in a chest that was panting with want. I pressed my thighs together again.

Something was not right.

I was not alone.

I reached under my pillow for the dagger I always kept near. Beside the steel of my blade, I felt a rough, long-fingered hand.

Someone else was in my bed.

6

S *iebold*

I WAS DREAMING. I lay in a soft bed, with a sweet-smelling woman in my arms. I dipped my head and breathed in the scent of her soft dark skin. Honey and spices. Enough to drive a man mad.

But I was already mad, wasn't I? This was a dream. A pleasant one.

I shifted my hand and palmed the thick thatch of hair between the maid's thighs. Slowly, my fingers stroked her folds until her arousal ran between my fingers. My other hand cupped her soft breast until her nipple beaded.

It'd been so long since I've been with a woman. So long since I dreamed of one. The last time--

No, I would not think of that. There was no madness buzzing in my mind. Only a pleasant armful. For once, the madness had given me a good dream.

My cock was hard enough to ram through rock. If the dream lasted a bit longer, I'd roll the woman over and sink into her heat.

I opened my eyes to a regal head, crowned with a thick brown braid. It was her. The woman who glowed with the light of the sun. I'd met her on the path, and now I was in her bed and she was in my arms.

The woman turned to face me. Her beautiful face hovered in front of mine. She was a vision. But she was real.

She slammed her elbow into my nose.

I sputtered, my eyes watering with pain. This was no dream. I was awake, and I'd never been so happy in my life. I'd get to sink my teeth, my claws, my cock into this perfect slice of heaven.

As soon as I relieved her of the blade she had at my throat.

7

M eadhan

THERE WAS a man in my bed. A beautiful man. Hard and muscular, with a blond beard and more coarse blond hair on his scarred chest. The warrior from my vision. He was real. He'd touched me.

By Ceridwen, he'd touched me. He'd stroked me and I'd felt... I don't know what it was that I felt. Before a moment ago, I would've sworn that there was no such thing as a love potion. But whatever magic the wolfman had was potent enough to make my limbs shake. My blood simmered, molten honey.

He was big and hard all over. Everywhere. Too big. Too hard. I pressed the knife to his throat and his cock grew against my leg. His fingers might've been magic, but a cock so big would bring no joy. I glanced down. It was long and thick and hard and pointed at me.

"Wolf," I whispered, feeling his magic still in the air.

There was a metallic tint to it. Like the bitter taste left after sucking on a small cut at the fingertip.

He didn't deny my accusation. He didn't need to. His golden eyes blazed as he offered me a sharp, white-toothed grin, wide enough to swallow me whole.

To show him I was serious, I pressed my dagger down. He smiled and leaned in. Blood trickled down the blade. The man was crazier than the wolf.

"Me and," he rasped, his voice rough as if he hadn't spoken in a long time.

What was it about this man, his eyes, his body stretched under me that felt so familiar? That felt so right?

Without meaning to, I eased off the blade so he could speak.

"Mead...ahh."

"Mead?" I asked. "Are you thirsty?"

In automatic hospitality, I rose to go to get him a drink, but he stopped me, his hand clamping around my wrist. My knife was at his heart now. But he ignored it. His eyes bored into mine. He took a deep breath and tried his hand at words again.

"Mead Ann."

With his other hand he reached out and touched the center of my chest. I realized he was saying my name.

I raised my chin. "Yes, my name is Meadhan. How did you know?" I answered my own question. "You followed me."

A quirk appeared in the corner of his mouth. "And you? What's your name?"

"See bowl."

I looked around for a bowl. He took my hand and

pressed it against his chest. Under my palm, his heart beat strong.

"Siebold," he said again. His growl reverberated up my arm.

"Siebold," I repeated.

He grinned again. I bet many women fell for that grin. It certainly worked on me. Here I was, facing a naked stranger, a very muscular, very blond stranger but a stranger none-theless, and I was exchanging conversation like we were at market. But it felt right.

I checked the power within me, but it lay quiet. Not suppressed, but expectant. Eager, but content to wait.

I set the knife to the side, on the bed. Siebold's grin grew wider. He was so handsome I felt dizzy. His charm a thousand times more dangerous than a village man's, if only because Siebold was so much more dangerous. His body was large, made entirely of honed muscle. Magic fairly crackled between us. I froze. Does he know that I'm a witch? *Kin knows kind*, my mother used to say. Something drew him to me when he was a wolf.

Maybe that's all this was. He felt the strangeness in me, and couldn't stay away.

His attention was fixed entirely on me now. Like I was the only woman in the world.

His hand cupped my face. His fingers were rough with healed cuts and calluses, but they were nimble and gentle as they explored my cheek.

I couldn't forget, he was no longer a feral wolf, but a naked man. The latter was far more dangerous and much less desirable to me.

I made to rise again. But again he held me firm.

"Let go," I demanded and glanced at the knife. Something told me that, when it came to this warrior wolf who fought off a gang of mercenaries as easy as scattering chickens, a small knife would be an ineffectual weapon.

"Stay," he said. It didn't sound like a plea. More of a command.

"You are an uninvited guest in my house."

"Welcome... here." He spread his hands over my mattress.

"When I thought you were a wounded animal. And not in my bed."

He grinned. Apparently he had no problem with comprehension. His words were becoming clearer the more he used his voice. How long had he been in wolf form?

He dipped his nose into my neck and inhaled. "Smell so good."

My skin prickled but not with danger. I kept my tone dry. "You're not going to eat me, are you?"

He pulled away and smiled. Flashing those canines. For some reason I felt no fear.

He reached up again. But this time for my hair.

I slapped his hand away before he could touch my braided curls. The pale men and women of these lands were always fascinated by them. "Don't touch my hair," I said as I patted my head to check my braids. Then I cursed. They'd come loose in the night. Likely his doing.

He laughed when I glared at him and then he captured my chin in between his fingers.

"Meadhan," he sighed.

The cadence of his speech was becoming clearer. His words were slightly accented, and guttural as if he was unused to a human tongue. The low rumble of his voice thrilled me.

It was no matter. I had to get him out of my bed. Out of my house. The last thing I needed was to be associated with a man who could become a wolf.

Siebold's grin fell into a fierce scowl. His head whipped to the door before I heard the visitor's approach.

Fear clouded my vision. Magic was one thing. I was an unmarried woman. If I wanted to keep my respectability and not have all manner of men reaching up my skirts, whoever was at the door could not find a man in my bed.

I shoved the naked man out the back and pulled on the wrap. "Stay," I hissed at him as if he were a dog. His jaw set as if he would argue and I panicked. "I'm serious. I cannot be seen with a strange man in my home."

His belligerent look fell away and he nodded.

Relieved, I shook out my braids and I opened the door, striding into my garden to face the men at my garden gate. A sickness crawled over my skin.

They were not from the village. I knew every face of every man from the village. I wish I could say these men were strangers. These were Offa the Bloody's men.

"We came to check on you," said the tall one. "After the incident with the wolf last night."

"I'm fine, as you can see," I said. "Did one of your men need an herbal remedy?"

They looked me up and down. Herbs were not what they wanted.

"You're far out of town," said one who was missing most of his teeth. "A pretty little thing like you needs a man's protection."

My dagger was back on the bed. My best chance to avoid any assault was to keep them on the other side of the gate. I could run to my hut, shut the door quickly and scramble out the back, and lose them in the forest. I kept a board loose in a corner, just so I could escape.

In a flash of panic, I thought of all this. But I didn't think of Siebold until a golden wolf streaked around me.

"No," I gasped, but too late. The wolf stood between me and the men, his statue dwarfing them.

Offa's soldiers were all mean looking warriors, but they startled when faced with a giant wolf. The wolf growled low in his belly making the ground rumble. The men reached for their weapons, already backing away.

"He's harmless," I lied, moving swiftly to Siebold's side. Whether I was protecting the wolf from the interlopers or them from him, I wasn't sure.

"That's the wolf from last night. He wounded Emyr," one muttered.

"He followed me home. He's harmless to me," I kept my voice cool. "I can't promise the same to others."

Siebold's ears flattened and he growled louder. The sound rumbled through me and made me bold.

"Calm down," I ordered as if he would listen to me. But he was already pushing past me, planting his huge body between me and the men. He plopped right down on my radishes, but I didn't complain. I tried to tug him back, but when he wouldn't budge, I settled for running my hands through his fur, and he relaxed somewhat.

"What is it you men came here for?" I asked. I couldn't get rid of Siebold, so I'd try to get these men to leave. With any luck, before blood was shed.

The men's gazes flicked between me and the wolf, mostly fixed on the wolf. *Please, just leave,* I prayed. I was a strange woman living alone in the forest, now with a pet wolf. The last thing I needed was word traveling back to the village about my strangeness. Eventually people would stop tolerating me and come as a mob to cast me out.

Kill the witch! The cries echoed in my memories and I bent my head to hide a shudder, digging my hands in Siebold's fur.

"Offa the Bloody has claimed this valley," the spokesman said slowly, reluctantly. "He's sworn to protect the folk who live here."

"Mmmm. What does that have to do with me? I need no protection, as you can see."

"We were hired by the priest," another blurted.

"Hired to do what?" My stomach lurched but I kept myself calm.

"To root out any magic or witchcraft."

"I don't believe in either," I said. "You'll find nothing here but the herbs that God put here." I pulled my cloak about my shoulders.

At my feet, Siebold growled.

"You might not believe, but you'll still pay for our protection," the spokesman jerked his chin up. "All villagers must."

So that was what this was really about. That was how it began in my mother's old village as well. Hopefully, if everyone paid, they would leave us all alone. Otherwise, I would have to go on the run once more.

"How much?" I asked, and they told me a sum. I pursed my lips as if considering it. The amount didn't matter, I knew it would increase.

One of the men grew impatient at my thoughtful silence, and stepped forward as if to threaten me. Instantly, Siebold was on his feet with a bowel-unhinging sound. His big body blocked my view, but the scrambling boots told me my visitors were leaving.

"We'll be back," the last one shouted before disappearing into the forest.

As I rose to my feet, my heart plummeted to the ground. The men would be back and bring reinforcements. Again and again until there were too many to drive away. Warrior wolf or not, I'd be driven from my land and my home.

I would not celebrate. This was a bleak day. The wolf had won me two battles, but in the end we'd lose the war.

8

S *iebold*

I TROTTED the perimeter of Meadhan's land, pausing every so often to cock a leg and mark a tree. Any wise predator would scent this territory was mine.

The men who'd threatened Meadhan had gone. I hadn't comprehended their words at first. I was too intent on the offense of their presence too near to her. Their eyes had roamed over her. Their breath had come too close to her sweet scent.

I still didn't understand why I'd left their throats intact. Especially since Meadhan now smelled like sadness.

"You can't stay," she'd said after they'd gone. "If they find out what you are they will kill you. If you are near me when they discover your secret, they'll kill me too." Then she'd swayed into the hut and shut the door. Shut me out.

Her problem was simple enough to solve. The men made her sad, so I'd kill them all.

Then Meadhan would be safe and she'd welcome me into her hut once more and I could spend my days with my face buried between her thighs, resting in the valley between her breasts, sipping at those lush lips as she cried out in pleasure.

I had a plan.

I nosed around a great pine tree and raised my leg to coat it in my scent, when I caught a whiff of raw meat. Perhaps Meadhan had come out to break her fast with me. I let my stream spatter the trunk, then crouched and willed the Change to come. I'd defended her as a wolf, but it was time for Meadhan to see me again as a man. She needed to get used to me.

Pain rippled down my spine, but the Change refused to come. I clawed the earth and tried again, but I remained on all fours.

In my former life, it was easier to change between man and wolf. I'd let the beast free for so many years I had forgotten how to be a man. It was going to take me some time to shift back now.

It was no matter. I had no plans to be anywhere else.

I was heading back to the hut when I caught the strange scent. Meat, fresh, wrapped in cabbage leaves, but carried by a man. A stranger.

I broke from the forest at the back of the hut just as a man loped out of the woods, carrying the food in his hands like an offering. He was tall, smiling. Eager. He strolled up to the garden gate and entered like he owned it.

My hackles rose as I watched the dead man walking onto my woman's land.

9

M*eadhan*

"Mistress Meadhan."

My head snapped up at the deep voiced greeting. Donna's son stood just inside my garden gate, a dimpled smile on his face.

I brushed chaff from my skirt and rose. "Good morn, sir." What was his name? A-something... "Alwyn. How are you today? How is your mother?"

"She is well, as am I. She bid me bring you--" he was already proffering the meat, walking towards me when a flash of fur caught the corner of my eye. The wolf charging Alwyn.

"No," I screeched and threw myself onto the wolf's back, my arms around its ruff. It dragged me forward a few feet before it stopped.

"Run, miss!" Alwyn ordered. He'd dropped the meat and

drawn a long knife. His face was pale under his brown beard, but to his credit, he hadn't backed down. "This beast is wild."

"No...he's mine. A stray. He obeys my every command. Sit," I tried to keep the pleading note out of my voice.

Siebold dropped his haunches onto the ground, but kept the snarl that showed his teeth.

"Stay," I said, praying to every goddess I knew that the wolfman would listen. "Down," I lowered my hand. With bristling fur and a baleful glare, Siebold lowered his body to the ground.

"See, he listens to me." I blew out a breath and resisted the urge to wipe the sweat from my brow.

"I suppose so," Alwyn said slowly, easing back but still holding his knife. "What breed is he?"

We both looked at the great blond body lying at my feet. The wolf's legs were curled under him as if any second he could spring into attack. I knew if Alwyn moved toward me, he would.

"A...wolf dog." Siebold's ears twitched towards me. *Dog?*

I heard the word clearly in my mind. I sucked in a breath and Alwyn looked at me sharply. Did he sense I was hearing voices?

The wolf's gaze was still on Alwyn, his lip curled away from his teeth a fraction more.

"Er, hound," I amended. "A mountain wolf hound. From my mother's country."

Alwyn nodded politely. "I beg pardon. I didn't know he was...tame." He sheathed his knife and moved slowly to pick up the fallen meat. "Apologies, Mistress--"

"I'll wash it. It'll be fine. Please convey my thanks to your mother." I stepped forward and reached for the gift, and Siebold the mountain wolf hound blocked me.

I sighed and said to Alwyn, "Leave it on the gate post, if you will."

Reluctantly, Alwyn left the package where I bid, said farewell, and left.

"You," I rounded on Siebold as soon as Alwyn was safely out of hearing. "Bad, bad dog. You don't bite my friends."

Friend?

This time the word echoed clearly in my head. I wasn't crazy. The wolfman could speak into my mind.

The wolf put a paw on the hem of my skirt and butted his head against my hip, asking to be petted.

"Yes, friend, you overgrown beast." I wrenched my skirts out from under his paw and batted him aside. "I can't believe you were so rude." I hustled to get the meat, but a streak of tan fur beat me to the gate. In a blur, the wolf snatched the bundle down in his jaws.

"No," I shouted, too late. With a sharp toss of his head, Siebold snapped the meat into the air, and swallowed it whole. I stood in wide-eyed disbelief as his huge jaws closed. A gulp and the meat was gone.

Tastes of cabbage. Blech.

I stomped my foot. "That was my meat! You ate my meat!"

You didn't want that meat.

"I most certainly did!"

Very well, Mistress Meadhan. The voice murmured, smug. *You shall have meat. I will fetch it.* The wolf started to trot away, pausing to look back and order, *Lock the gate and do not open it for any man. I will soon return.* And he disappeared into the forest, leaving me glaring in his wake.

∾

"STUPID MEN," I hissed, hacking at the raspberry brambles in an untamed corner of my garden. "Always wanting to take over." I tossed my hoe aside and grabbed the little green runners, tugging them violently. They resisted, clinging to the earth. And I was done.

My power bubbled up out of me. Heat struck my skin as if I'd bent too close to a fire. I yelped. Light sparked from my fingers, flaring like a match--a shocking blaze and then it was out, leaving me trembling.

Scorched earth extended in a perfect circle around my feet. The fire hadn't harmed anything beyond a small section. My cucumbers were untouched. But the stray briars were burnt to a crisp.

"Ceridwen help me." I stared at my hands, then tucked them under my chin. My gaze darted around, even though no one was near. I'd built my hut in the wild for a reason. No one would ever see me use my magic. Not that I used my powers often. Usually I kept it locked up tight, in the darkest corner of my heart.

Now it was threatening to break free. It had never been so unruly, not even when I was a girl. I'd chained it up like a dog, but it was a wild wolf now. It would never be tamed.

Like Siebold.

"This is all his fault," I muttered, running a hand over my braids. My hair crackled as if each strand contained power. Scuffing the earth so the perfect circle was marred, I marched to the front of my home and leaned over a water barrel. The reflection showed a mad woman, wide-eyed and wild-haired. If Mistress Donna and her son saw me now, they'd know what I was, and forget any friendship. They themselves would call for the priest and Offa's men to hunt me down.

What was I going to do?

A twig snapped and I jumped as a monstrous form emerged from the forest. When it stepped into the light I could make out what I was seeing: a man carrying a giant buck slung over his shoulders. A lesser man would've staggered under the weight, but this man easily maneuvered around a few bushes and strode right up to my garden gate where I stood with my mouth open. Then he lifted the buck off his shoulders and let the giant body crash at my feet.

"There," Siebold tossed his shaggy blond head and grinned at me. "Meat."

He looked as pleased as a boy who'd built his first fire. I should've examined the buck, but my eyes were only for the muscled warrior standing before me. He was totally naked.

My stomach did a slow, lazy flip. His beard was short but unkempt, a few white hairs threaded with the blond. But his body was young and strong, if a bit hairy. The hard-muscled plane of his chest was lightly furred with coarse blond hair. The hair trailed from his taut lower belly and ended in a bush between his legs, surrounding his giant cock.

And I was staring. I was staring at his cock.

I forced my gaze back up to his face, where Siebold's smile had turned wicked.

"Meadhan," his voice was a purr. He started towards me and then stopped short to sniff the air. His eyes narrowed. "Magic." His head swiveled towards the back of the house and then to me. His irises shone bright gold.

"It's nothing," I said quickly. "A mishap." I hid my hands in my skirts. "Was it a good hunt?"

He crossed his arms over his chest. *You tell me.*

"Don't do that," I muttered, shaking my head as if gnats were buzzing around my ears. "Don't speak into my mind."

Meadhan. You needn't hide from me.

"You need clothes." I ducked my head and hustled to the

hut, returning with a leather hide, cured until it turned soft. He took it and fashioned a loincloth around his hips. The scrap of leather barely covered his powerful buttocks. I tried not to stare.

And failed. And of course he caught me at it.

"Meadhan--"

"Thank you for covering yourself." I rubbed my hands in my skirts and stepped around the buck's extensive antlers. "We should do something with the kill."

In answer, Siebold strode to the side of my hut and took up an axe. "Fire. Spit."

We worked together to raise and drain the buck, and lay wood for a bonfire. Each of Siebold's moves taxed the loincloth to its limit. And when he lifted the buck, his muscles stood out sleek and shiny with sweat, and the loincloth also lifted to reveal what was underneath.

Not that I noticed.

Having a huge warrior around to help lift and chop and carry things was handy. A few swings of his axe and we had a whole tree downed for a fire. Not to mention the giant buck.

I wouldn't need to forage for food for a while, I realized as the pile of wood rose. We could feast for days and then dry the meat. I could live out here with my pet warrior wolf and pretend the village wasn't near. Never return...

A shadow fell over my face as Siebold stepped close. He studied my face, his golden eyes teasing out secrets until I felt bare before him.

"What do you want?" I sniped, raising my chin. This is why I never kept a man. Most were too intimidated by a woman who challenged them instead of folding herself into something smaller to make them feel large and important. I would not do it. I refused to make myself small.

Siebold's grin told me my defiance did not cow him. He stepped closer, and closer still, even when I folded my arms across my chest. Fool warrior must have a death wish.

"My meat. My kill." He gestured to the hanging buck. I looked to it and back to him several times before I understood.

"Oh, I see. You want me to say you're the better hunter. That I like your meat better than any other man's." I blushed as I said it.

He cocked his head. *Yes.* His voice slipped into my head, teasing.

"I won't do it. How do I know this meat is better? I haven't tasted it."

Yet. He smirked, cocky as a god.

"Maybe I'll never taste it. Maybe I don't eat meat."

A hint of insecurity slipped into his smile.

"Maybe I prefer mushrooms," I went on. He stared at me a moment, then pivoted and walked towards the forest. Heading off, no doubt, to find the largest mushroom in the forest for me.

"Wait!" I threw myself at him. He let me grab his arm and drag him back. "I merely jested. I like meat. I will eat it."

He turned, grinning again. Somehow I was in his arms, plastered against his broad chest. His shoulders flexed under my hands as he lifted me and carried me easily back to the fireside.

"Meat," he grunted, stopping by the fire but refusing to let me down. "Mine."

I threw back my head and heaved a large sigh to hide the fact that I was enjoying the feel of his arms around my body. "Very well. Yours is the best meat. The only meat for me."

He looked so smug I couldn't keep back my laugh or my smile.

"Mine," he huffed again and loosened his hold so I slid slowly down his body. The loincloth did nothing to soften the hard ridges of his body. His eyes held mine, his gaze like a torch, igniting sparks in the secret places of my sex.

A flush came over me. A wind rose and whirled around us, lifting his hair, tugging at my braids. Then it was gone, and I realized how much dirt and ash clung to my hands, my dress.

Siebold was also filthy. He stank of blood and the hunt. We both did.

"I need to wash," I muttered.

Siebold lifted his grimy hands as if to say *So do I.*

"There's a waterfall nearby, with a deep pool." A part of me knew it was dangerous to invite him, but I couldn't help it.

Siebold regarded me a moment before lifting his head to scent the wind. *Show me.*

10

S *iebold*

MEADHAN WALKED LIKE A CAT, graceful and precise, never making a sound. We strolled side by side. She took two and a half steps for one of my strides, but never seemed to hurry or fall behind. My body still thrummed, remembering how she felt in my arms. Her scent rose around me, a rich herbal fragrance my wolf wanted to bask and roll around in.

When the path turned, she signaled me to follow her lead. She was careful not to touch me. But when I held her, I felt her body respond. I frighten and intrigue her. She would not be easy prey, but no matter. I am a patient hunter.

As soon as we came to the pool, deep and clear to the rocky bottom, I strode out in front and pulled off my loincloth.

This time she did not hide the fact that she was watching.

I faced her and held out my hand.

"Oh no," she shook her head and pointed to the far end of the pool. "I'll bathe over there."

I didn't move. She held my stare but a red tinge started to creep up her glossy brown cheeks. I raised a brow in dare.

"This is a mistake," she finally muttered and loosened her apron while kicking off her shoes.

I'd won, but I didn't press the matter. I turned my back to give her privacy, and leapt into the pool.

The freezing shock made me roar. I surged out of the water, gasping.

Meadhan was laughing, a low chuckle that sent rivulets of warmth to my cock despite the freezing cold. I did a few strokes, swimming briskly to warm up. If I stayed in any longer, my cock was going to shrivel up and fall off.

Then I turned and caught a glimpse of a forest nymph, long legs and rounded buttocks, dark brown skin flashing and braids flying as she flew through the air and crashed into the water. The perfection of her made my heart stutter.

Her face broke the surface. "C-c-c-eridwen, it's cold," she gasped.

I reached for her before I could stop myself. She let me gather her into my arms and share what little warmth I had. Our bodies fit together perfectly.

"Your lips are blue," she brushed cold fingers over my mouth. I tried to kiss her and she pushed me away. "Who-ever can hold their breath the longest wins," she cried. She gulped a huge breath and dove.

I followed, my head bursting from the cold. When I opened my eyes, she was swimming away, her long body lithe as a mermaid. I tried to follow but had to surface for air.

Meadhan had disappeared behind the waterfall. She'd

sat up on a rock and drawn her long legs up to her chest, and was combing out her hair with her fingers. She looked so regal and serene, a daughter of the forest, a ray of warm sunlight, calm and perfect and lovely.

And I knew: I'd searched for this woman for a century. Now that I'd found her, I would never let her go.

The wild cry of the hunt echoed in my mind, a howling long and melancholy as a wolf's song.

And the beast within broke its chain.

11

M *eadhan*

SIEBOLD ROSE UP BEFORE ME, water running over his golden muscles. He was wet and wild-eyed as a river god.

"What--" I started to ask when he leaned down and stopped my mouth with his. For a moment I let his lips speak for him. His beard brushed my face. Other than that, he didn't touch me, but I sensed the coiled energy inside him. He would catch me if I tried to run.

I wasn't going to run. I wrapped my arms around him and he lifted me, his mouth never leaving mine. My legs hooked around his hips and tugged him even closer.

He slipped on the rocks and we fell into the waterfall. The rush of water made me throw my head back, breaking the kiss, but Siebold found his balance and steadied us away from the flow. He chased my lips with a growl. He kissed up the column of my neck, finding my pulse and sucking on it until my body clenched.

Mine, a voice howled in my head. It was a savage cry, feral and achingly lonely. *Mine. Mine. Mine.* It wasn't Siebold, and it was. The dark monster living inside him, born of the curse and doomed to forever feel a hunger no hunt could satisfy.

I knew this monster, because one lived inside me as well. And as Siebold gripped me hard enough to bruise and claimed my lips again, she broke free.

The wind rushed around us, making goosebumps rise on our flesh. We didn't notice. I surged against Siebold, digging my nails into his shoulders. He snarled and captured my mouth again. We danced and fought in each other's arms on the edge of the waterfall, ignoring the crashing cold.

Eventually Siebold's feet slipped again and we fell. We burst from the pool and sought each other again. The cold was gone, replaced by the *boom boom boom* of my heartbeat and the aching lust in my loins.

He was naked, I was ready, but I wouldn't let him go long enough for me to guide him inside me. And he wouldn't break the kiss. So I rocked against him, finding as much stimulation against his hard midriff as I could, while he kissed and kissed and kissed me like I was pure water and he was dying of thirst.

I don't know what caught my attention first. The creaking branches? A hiss of steam? I opened my eyes as a mighty wind tore through the trees, whipping them until they tossed their leafy heads. All around us was chaos. Rocks overturned, tumbling into the pool. Tree limbs crashed to the ground, surrendered to the wind.

And the water around us was warm. Steam rose from the edges.

I jerked up out of the water as if it burned. Siebold grunted, but opened his eyes, and took in my wide-eyed shock.

Meadhan. You're glowing.

I held out my hands. Sure enough, light danced along my wrists, haloing my brown skin.

My power was out of control. And I might never coax it back into hiding. It wouldn't fit into the small dark corner of my heart. It'd grown too large.

I clutched my hair, calling my power back. Begging for control. By the time Siebold carried me out of the water and set me down, the wind had died. The light around my skin faded. But the broken branches and upturned rocks bore evidence of what my power had done.

I swallowed and flinched when Siebold turned from surveying the mess. But he didn't look frightened. He pulled me close and brushed his lips over my forehead, then pulled back and cupped my face.

He saw me, saw what I could do, like no one else.

"I've never felt anything like that," I whispered.

Neither have I.

12

S *iebold*

BY UNSPOKEN AGREEMENT, we spoke not a word to each other as we returned to Meadhan's home. I chopped more wood and built a spit while she skinned the buck and butchered it. She removed some entrails for her own preparation and I secured the rest of the carcass over the fire. The work left us bloody, but this time we washed separately in a nearby stream.

When I returned from cleaning up, I joined Meadhan by the fire. We stood shoulder to shoulder a long moment, tension crackling between us. She'd accepted my touch by the waterfall. My beast did not frighten her. If anything, I should fear her power. But any fear I would have was driven out of me by desire.

I reached down and took her hand. Her fingers slender and graceful, soft in a way that belied how strong she was.

In the darkness of the night's sky, her brown skin was radiant. When I turned her hand over, her palm was pale with a hint of white and pink. Her knuckles were darker where the skin creased. I kissed them and the heat of her skin shot through me, calling the beast. When she glanced up and met my eyes, I knew they shone gold.

"I should go," she said on a shaky breath. "The meat will be a while. I need to...rest."

She pulled her hand from my grip, picked up her skirts and practically ran, leaving me thoughtful.

I hunkered down and stretched my hand out towards the fire. The heat steadied me. The beast within should be snarling and slavering at its cage bars, but it too was silent. Steady. Patient. Ready to pounce.

Soon, I promised it, and turned my thoughts to our prey. Meadhan acted cold towards me, but she had not cast me out, even though she had the power to do so. She also welcomed me, in her own prickly way. And when she was warm towards me, she was more than warm. Her blood ran hot, searing me from the inside out.

I smirked into the fire, remembering. A part of her wanted me. But it might take longer to seduce my little witch. The last emotion I scented on her was fear. And it was not me she feared, but her own desire.

13

M eadhan

I STRETCHED out on my bed, determined to calm myself. After a minute I flopped over one way, then the other.

My bed was too hard. My hut was too cold. My body, too warm.

This was Siebold's fault.

I should curse him, and turn him into a toad. But whenever I tried to still my thoughts as my mother taught me, the memory of our bodies entwined sent simmering waves washing through my limbs.

Now my blankets, my skirts, my very skin were too hot. I leapt up and grabbed a scrap of cloth, dunked it in the bucket and wrung it out. I wiped down my neck, my throat, my chest. My breasts felt different, swollen. Ripe fruit, ready for a hot mouth to nibble and suck and devour.

"This isn't happening to me," I muttered and lay back

down. Yesterday morn I'd been fully in control of my flesh and my powers. One warrior couldn't destroy my hard-earned calm.

I relaxed on my bed, the cloth a cool weight covering my eyes. I steeled my mind and began the breathing exercises my mother taught me.

"Oi, leggo! Help!"

A horrible sound disturbed my meditation. I snatched the cloth off my face and sprang off the bed. In a single bound, I crossed the room and raced out the door.

Outside my garden gate, the huge blond wolf tussled with a ragged bundle. Once I was closer, I made out the dirty-faced boy, the source of the frightened shouting.

"Siebold, let him go," I motioned. The wolf opened its jaws and the boy tumbled back into the dirt. I recognized him then.

"Dafydd? What are you doing here?" By the looks of him, he hadn't visited Mistress Donna and gotten his promised meal. His eyes were sunken into his face, and he stared at the roasting buck.

"Came to see where the witch lived," the boy muttered.

I kept my face expressionless, though inwardly I flinched when he called me the witch. Siebold rumbled. The boy glanced at the wolf, flashing the whites of his eyes.

"It's all right. He won't hurt you." I picked up my skirts and swept between them. "I won't allow it."

"It's a wolf," said Dafydd.

"Yes." I gathered my calm in a fist and tried not to wonder why the day I woke with a warrior in my bed I had three more sets of visitors. "How's your leg?"

The boy shrugged and lifted his healed leg for my inspection. "Better."

I stayed where I was, between the boy and the wolf. "Good."

"I know you did something." He stood, dusting off his hands. "I didn't tell anyone."

A fact I was grateful for, but no telling how long it would last. "Where do you live, Dafydd?"

"In the forest. Behind the midden."

That explained the smell.

"Folks don't bother me there," he added, kicking a stick into the fire. He couldn't stop looking at the roasting deer, though he kept darting nervous glances at the wolf. "Is he tame?"

We both looked at Siebold, who cocked his head at me. Challenging me to answer.

"No," I said firmly. "You can never tame a wild beast. But he is mine. As long as he is here," I amended. "As long as he stays, he is mine." I held out my hand and Siebold trotted over, rubbing his head against my palm. I hid my surprise, and turned my attention back to the boy.

He was too skinny. But he was almost as tall as me. Give him more food and he'd shoot up like a weed. Maybe even be taller than one of Donna's sons.

"Would you like some meat, Dafydd?"

The boy swallowed and nodded.

"I'll slice some off for you. But first you must wash." I went to fetch the water myself, dipping a bucket into the large barrel I kept to catch the rain. I added a few sprigs of lavender and hyssop. It wouldn't do much, but might help a little with the fleas.

Dafydd eyed the bucket as if it was full of dung. "Priest says washing is evil. It lets the demons in."

"Do you believe that?" I left him with the bucket and

picked up my long knife and whetstone. I sharpened the blade with long strokes.

"Dunno. Got no reason not to."

"Do you believe everything the priest says is true?"

"He's my da."

"Then why doesn't he take care of you?"

"Priests can't have sons." The boy said it bravely, but a little quaver in his chin told me how many times he'd been reviled and cast out. How he clung to the quirk of human law and birth that left him hungry and neglected most of his life.

"Where is your mother?"

"Got sick and dead. Fever. She tole me who my da was, but Father Gerald won't take me in."

Father Gerald should die, I thought savagely, running my knife along the whetstone.

"If you were my boy, I'd claim you. I'd give you a bed to sleep in and feed you often so you would grow. But you'd have to wash first." I looked pointedly at the bucket. Then I went to the buck and started carving the first choice bits of burnt flesh. Siebold the wolf came to stand beside me, large and silent.

The boy joined us soon after, still dripping. From the look of it, he'd plunged his whole head in the water.

"Priest says I got demons in me anyway, 'cause I'm a bastard," he said cheerfully, and accepted a strip of meat.

I fed him slowly, watching him for any signs of hunger sickness. For a while he ate quickly and neatly, his eyes fixed on the next scrap. When his cheeks flushed with color and his chewing slowed, I had him sip some mead, my own brew, and sit a while while I carved off a large hank.

I forgot Siebold was hovering close until he darted in

and snapped up the bone I was cleaving, dancing away before I could catch him.

"He's quick," Dafydd observed.

"Yes. And he knows he needn't steal." I put my hand on my hip, resisting the urge to lecture Siebold. I would not be the madwoman talking to a wolf like he was a man. No need to add to the stories of my strangeness. "None go hungry at my hearth."

I went to carve more meat and saw Dafydd eyeing the roast again, even though he'd edged back to a rock closer to the forest than to the fire.

"You are welcome here anytime, Dafydd." The boy might hold my secret forever, or be my downfall, but I could not let him starve. "We don't always eat so well but--"

Siebold barked. I sighed.

"As long as I have the wolf, we will have meat. The wolf is a good hunter."

Another bark.

"The best hunter," I threw up my hands. The wolf snuffed in contentment and went back to gnawing his bone. My exasperation with Siebold died when I caught a smile hovering in the corner of Dafydd's mouth.

The rest of the afternoon, we lounged by the fire and ate like kings. The boy's belly grew round, but he never refused a fresh scrap of meat. But he wouldn't move closer to the fire, even when I coaxed him and offered him a blanket, in hopes he would fall asleep and spend the night. But he refused.

It didn't surprise me, though inwardly I mourned. All children deserve love and care. But the boy was half feral. Not unlike the wolf. Or me.

Sometime between twilight and dark, Dafydd slipped away. I cleaned up, banking the fire and carrying the bucket back to the garden. I dropped more herbs into the water barrel. If Dafydd returned, perhaps I could get him to wash again.

"He'll be back," a deep voice startled me. Siebold the man stepped out from behind the hut.

"What are you doing?" I hissed. "Bad enough Dafydd saw you as the wolf. He can't see that I have a man."

I grabbed his arm and marched him to my door. Bulging with muscle as he was, it shouldn't have been so easy to drag Siebold into my hut. I suspected it wouldn't be so easy to drag him somewhere he didn't want to go.

He dipped his head to enter my home. When he straightened, the space shrank. He was wearing the loincloth, but the sight of his bare body made my mouth dry and my body hungry all over again. He dwarfed me, and for a moment I imagined his long, lean, hard muscled body stretched over me. Naked. All that golden skin...

I put a hand to my neck to hide my flush. "I should not allow you in."

With a grin, he shut the door. *I'm already inside.* He didn't mean my hut. He stepped towards me, ducking to avoid a bundle of herbs.

"Oh no," I pointed to the far corner. "You sleep over there."

"Meadhan," he murmured. He took my hand, turned it palm up and kissed it. I felt the brush of his lips all the way to my cunny.

"Why were you cursed?" I blurted. His face went blank. The light flickered in his eyes and died. Something inside me died too, but now I was curious. "What matter of man were you to seek out a witch and accept that sort of spell?"

He turned away and crouched near the fire, striking a

flint to light it. He held his hand over the small flame, nurturing it until it grew.

When his voice came it was almost too low for me to hear. "I was a warrior. The witch promised our king power. She would use her magic to turn us into great warriors. Only the best were chosen."

"You were chosen."

"Yes."

I sat on the bed and tucked my skirts around me. Now that Siebold wasn't standing close, I was left chilled. "Spells like that have a way of turning on the recipient," I said to fill the silence. "Magic always comes with a price."

"We knew it would. It did not matter. I would become bigger, stronger, faster. Nothing else mattered." He passed a hand over his face. "I did not know it would bar me from Valhalla."

"How do you mean?"

He raised his head and his eyes blazed brighter than the fire. "We cannot die. The beast rages within us. We are all powerful. Berserkers."

I licked my lips, my heart pounding as if I was in the presence of a monster. "Surely there is a way to die."

"The Alpha might will it. A Berserker can kill a Berserker. But I was not granted a quick death. They cast me out of the pack. They were my brothers, and I betrayed them."

I remained quiet.

"I betrayed them," Siebold repeated. In my mind, a fierce cry echoed, haunting as a wolf's and full of despair. It died away and for long moments there was only the crackling of the fire. A question was on the tip of my tongue when Siebold continued.

"There was a warrior I followed. A leader. He left us and

sought out a priest. He even changed his name." His brow furrowed, and he crouched closer to the fire as if he could discern his own memories from the flames.

"Samuel," he said at last. "He changed his name to Samuel. I do not remember what he was called before."

Siebold turned and held out his hand, tipping it one way and then the other as if it was a level on a fulcrum. "There is a balance among a band of warriors. Our violence is tempered by discipline. By leadership. The leaders contain and direct us." He dropped his hand. "But Samuel left us. That was when the madness took hold."

'You blame him for your madness?"

"No. He did what he needed to do. Another warrior saved him. But it was too late for me."

"Too late?"

He tilted his head. "I thought it was. Until I met you."

14

S *iebold*

MY LITTLE WITCH sat on her bed, her hands folded neatly in her lap. She bowed her head, her brow furrowed as she weighed my words. "Why me?"

I shrugged. I could answer her, but not in words. How could I explain the weight of the curse, the pain, the constant darkness pressing over me like a cloud of flies? Her scent entered my world and pierced the veil. Because of her I could see the sun. But before the sun came in, she was my only light.

How could I explain this when I did not understand it myself?

"I don't know. It was that way with the Alphas of the pack. They found a woman and she soothed their beast. I cannot remember why." The years of running with a pack were all a blur. There was a sense of brotherhood, of oneness, even though I hovered on the outskirts. And then everything was severed. They cast me out to wander alone.

Meadhan pursed her lips, her brow furrowing further. "I could help you remember."

"No," I snapped. "Let those memories lie." The beast rose in me and I fought it. It did not want to remember.

Meadhan searched my face, and seemed to understand. "You chose madness over your memories."

"I've done much evil."

Slowly, she leaned down and dipped her fingers in the water jug, then rose and flicked the water over my face. I blinked.

"I absolve you," she said in her husky voice. "I forgive you for what you've done."

15

M eadhan

THE CREAKING floor was my only warning. The jug shattered at my feet, but I barely noticed because I was flat on my back, gazing up into feral eyes.

Siebold shifted his bulk over me, pinning me with his body, his gaze.

"You think you can absolve me," he snarled. His voice was twisted, monstrous. The beast off its chain.

"I can," I answered steadily. "And I did."

His nostrils flared. I freed a hand and passed it gently over his brow. My fingers slender and delicate stroking his skin. "Be at peace."

For a long moment, the blond warrior remained suspended over me, breathing hard. Then, in a rush, he was gone, standing across the room as far from me as he could go. Was it wrong that I felt the loss?

I smoothed my dress to hide my distress. My own heart fluttered. If the warrior was paying attention, he'd have known it was excitement not fear.

Siebold stood in the middle of the hut, staring at the door. Trapped in memories. He'd said more in this night than he had in days. Maybe years. I would let him think.

I collected my skirts and stooped to clean up the broken jug. The warrior still did not notice.

"You have much magic," he said after a long while. "It might be enough to bring me back. But it might not."

"It might not," I agreed.

"I should go."

I dropped the pieces of the jug and crossed the room swiftly. "You cannot go." I drew myself up to face him. My head barely came up to his neck. My body was slight before him, a reed before an oak. I looked too small to stop such a large warrior, but I was determined. "I will not let you."

"You would try to tame me, witch?" Siebold's voice was gruff, his eyes bright. I knew it wasn't the man who faced me, but the beast.

"No. You heard me tell Dafydd. No one can tame a wild wolf."

He reached out and splayed a hand over my collarbone. His long fingers stretched shoulder to shoulder, framing my neck. "I'm dangerous."

I leaned into his palm and whispered, "So am I." I let my own power rise. My hair lifted and my own eyes glowed. No sense hiding from him. "I won't forget what you are. Don't forget what I am. Tread softly, Siebold, and we will get along."

His head tilted and eyes narrowed as if he was puzzling out what I meant.

I made it clear. "You are not leaving."

His body relaxed. Suddenly, we stood together not as strangers, not as adversaries, but something more.

"No," he said and slowly raised his hand to brush my brow, mimicking my earlier movement. "I don't suppose I am."

16

S iebold

I CUPPED the back of Meadhan's neck, clamping my fingers tight. Not hurting, but holding her still. I searched her eyes, waiting for her to put up a fight.

She relaxed against me. Her mouth opened, lips parting in soft, sweet invitation.

"Tell me you want this," I growled. "Tell me to stay." But before she could answer, I dropped my head and took her lips. I gripped her nape, guiding her closer.

"Yes," she gasped against my mouth. "Yes."

Fire shot through me. I lifted her in my arms, and she twined herself around me, tugging me closer with her legs.

We fell back onto the bed, lips still drinking each other in. She wriggled and I realized she was struggling out of her dress. I grabbed the edge of the garment and tugged to help her. Her arms whipped over her head as her dress came free. Fabric tore.

"It's all right," my little witch said wildly. "I don't care." Her hands found my jaw, guiding me back to her mouth.

"Meadhan," her name rumbled in my throat. I tugged her into place below me. My cock jerked towards her heat, but I ignored it. I had to taste her. I kissed down her neck to her perfect breasts, where I could lick and suck and worship. Then my mouth moved lower still.

My little witch writhed under me, her nails scratching my sides. I pinned her hips and scooted down, following her heady scent to its source. Her dark thighs were wet and slick, dripping honey. I nuzzled there, rubbing my beard against her tender skin and making her wriggle. I eased her leg over my shoulder, spreading the other leg wide so she split open for me. Yes. This was where I would live.

My tongue danced over her folds, nipping her when she struggled, and rewarding her when she stilled by licking her until her legs shook. She cried and convulsed, digging her fingers into my hair. I rubbed my chin in the nest of her dark hair before bending my head to tease her to climax again. I ignored my cock, thick and angry and heavy as a club between my legs. Nothing mattered but Meadhan's scent and her lithe body, fighting and climaxing and tugging me closer, all at the same time.

Lightning flashed and thunder boomed, shaking the little hut. It blinded and deafened me. I groped in the darkness, grasping her face so I could claim her mouth. I thrust my tongue inside her mouth as I longed to do with my cock. Soon. First, I would let her body ease open for me.

A light blazed in the corner of the hut. The fire, finding new life. I blinked. Meadhan had her hand outstretched, muttering. A few logs rolled from their stack into the fire.

Her midnight skin glowed in the firelight. I dug my fingers into the soft cloud of her hair, tugging her head back. My mouth covered the sensitive spot on her neck, sucking until she squirmed. My lips left a red mark, right where my woman should bear a mating mark.

A growl rumbled in my chest. The beast approved.

Still, I wanted to take my time, to savor her. With my fingers still in her hair, I tugged at the end of one plait. This time, she did not slap my hand away from her tresses. She allowed me to unravel first one and then another of her braids. It was as though I were undressing her all over again. When her crown of curls were free I gathered a handful and gave her head a tug. Her neck was bared to me.

I kissed my way down her throat to her bared breasts, lovely brown mounds like a strong brew of mead topped with darker nipples. I had to taste them.

I lapped at the tightened buds, circling them with my tongue. Goosebumps rose over her flesh, and I had to taste those too. Her heated skin gave off a rich, honeyed scent that made my cock throb. But I ignored my painful arousal and moved my mouth over Meadhan, worshipping her perfection.

"Siebold," she clawed at my shoulders. "Siebold, please."

I kissed back up her body. She grunted, her fingers digging into my skin, impatient as she tried to maneuver me over her. I hitched her leg up and she wrapped her calf around my buttocks, pulling me towards her. I lowered myself into the cradle of her hips, groaning as her fingers found my iron hard length. She stroked me in her palm once, twice, then guided me home.

She was all tightness and slick heat, her skin silken under my rough palms.

Meadhan moaned in my arms and a red film washed over my vision. The beast was taking over.

I threw back my head and roared.

17

M eadhan

A FIERCE WIND howled outside the hut. Siebold's canines glinted over me. For a moment, my Sight flashed with a vision of a monstrous beast, its jaws wide to bite its prey. I'd allowed this warrior into my home, my bed and body.

My mother's tale of the wolfman told me when a wolfman found his mate, he would mark her with a bite. The mark would never fade. My magic would heal me, but the mark would leave a scar, a sign I was a witch, plain for all to see.

"No," I shouted and threw my arm up. My power blasted the warrior backwards, but he fought it, his teeth snapping close. Grabbing him, I rolled us off the bed.

We landed with Siebold under me. Fur rippled down his arms and chest. His eyes glowed. He was a monster, but inside me was a wild thing, monstrous in her own way. I'd kept her hidden for years, but she would hide no longer. She was hungry, sensing the beast in Siebold. Her power licked at him and liked the taste.

The beast under me roared in my face and I snarled back. Power crackled along my limbs, blazing bright.

Our monsters stared at each other. His was bigger but mine was stronger.

Outside, a storm broke. Winds smashed into the hut, buffeting it. A trio of pots fell from my mantel to the hearth. The sound of their smashing was swallowed by the echoing thunder. Lightning sizzled just outside the door.

My hair stood on end. Small items rose around us, levitating a foot or two off the floor. The air was thick with my power.

Siebold opened his great jaws and lunged at me. I drove him back, my power pinning him to the floor.

"No. You will please me," I growled. I was still on top of him, straddling him. I gripped his shoulders and bore down, seating myself firmly on his thick rod. My hips rolled in a powerful rhythm.

Siebold bared his teeth at me, but the more I rocked over him, breasts bouncing, the less he seemed to mind me taking control. He seized my hips and snapped his own, driving his cock deeper inside me. I cried out and almost toppled over, but he propped me up, forcing me to ride him.

His hand encircled my throat. "Mine," he snarled.

"Mine," I snapped back and slid my own hands to his throat. It took both of mine to span the front of his powerful neck. A rumble rose from his chest, but he seemed content. His eyes grew heavy lidded and he drove his powerful body upwards, fucking me from below.

My own movements slowed, growing languid as pleasure shimmered through me. I leaned back and clutched his wrist. Holding on, holding him close as he collared my neck.

Outside the storm was still raging. Inside, a strange wind blew. The items in the air spun around us.

His hand tightened around my throat and I began to shake.

"Siebold," I shrieked to the ceiling as my pleasure claimed me. Something smashed in the corner. A bundle of herbs broke from its string and blew past my face. The door banged open and swung wildly, battered by the wind.

Under me, Siebold's body tightened. His hips surged upwards as he drove into me with a howl. His fingers tightened around my throat. A white blast seared my vision. Then there was a huge boom, a giant rush of air over my face.

And I knew no more.

18

M *eadhan*

I WOKE to sunlight hitting my face. My whole body screamed when I tried to move. "Ohh, mercy." My thighs and inner muscles were especially sore.

"Morning," Siebold murmured. He was grinning.

"You're happy," I grumbled. My head throbbed like I'd drunk a cask of mead.

"The sun is shining, I have a beautiful witch in my arms..."

"Shhhh," I pressed my fingers over his lips. "Don't say that. Supposed to be a secret."

"What, that you're beautiful?" Siebold brushed back the untamed cloud of my hair. "It's no secret."

"No, the other. Don't tell people I'm a witch."

His body did feel good, hard and warm, curled around mine. I shifted and realized we were still lying on the floor. We must have slept here all night. No wonder I was sore.

A bird fluttered down beside us, pecking at the floorboards. My eyes widened.

"Sorry, sweetness. That's no secret either. And if it is, not for long." Siebold waved a hand to shoo the bird away. It hopped aloft, fluttering upwards into the big, blue expanse of sky where my roof used to be, where it winged away.

"What have you done?" I launched myself up as well. My hut no longer had a roof. Herbs and pots lay strewn around the room, in a perfect circle from where Siebold and I had lain.

"Not me," Siebold rumbled. He caught me up in his arms, stepped over the broken pottery and herb bundles and carried me into the garden. The roof had blown off cleanly, the beams and rushes tossed into the forest as if by a giant hand.

At least it hadn't crushed my bean poles.

I dug my fingers into my hair, making it wilder than before. "I don't suppose this was the work of a sudden storm."

"A storm called Meadhan," Siebold said. He was still grinning. I could punch him.

At least I didn't live close to the village. If Offa's men or Mistress Donna's son visited me today, how would I explain it?

"I will fix it," Siebold promised. His arm slung around me, he tugged me into his side. I let him support me. He kissed my temple. "Do not worry. I will fix everything."

It was not the ruin of my hut I was most worried about. Or the fact that the warrior had moved so swiftly and completely into my life. It was getting harder to hide what I was.

My own power was free, and would no longer be tamed.

19

M eadhan

THE NEXT MORNING, I took the forest path that brought me around the village and deposited me directly into the field where people gathered for the market. My dress was long and modest despite the heat of the day, and my unruly hair was safely tucked under a covering. I looked the part of a demure village woman with a basket of herbal tinctures to sell.

"Just act as you always have," I ordered myself under my breath. "No one will guess the truth." No one would guess my body was still sore from the ardent attentions of a strange warrior. Or that the storm that'd swept through the forest and brought down branches all over the path had its origin with me. At least the worst of the damage was centered around my hut.

I smoothed my hand over my hair covering, straightened my bodice, and started to step from the forest into the light.

Only to stop short when a huge blond wolf blocked my way.

"Get back," I hissed. The wolf didn't obey. It stood in the middle of the path, using its body as a solid, furry wall to keep me back. "Siebold, I mean it."

The wolf spared me a brief glance, then swiveled its huge head back to study the market.

"It's fine. It's just the village market. I come here every week." I shifted my basket onto my hip, freeing up a hand to tug at his thick scruff. The wolf didn't budge. "You shouldn't even be here. I told you to wait back at the hut."

The wolf's lip curled. Then his whole body stilled. From the tip of its nose to the end of its tail, his body pointed like an arrow to some unseen threat in the market.

"What? What is it?"

Out in the market, a man walked between the stalls, using a stave to roll a barrel before him.

"Him? That's Cynog. He's fine. He makes mead." The man reached his stall and tugged the barrel upright. If he followed habit, he would tap the barrel and sample his own wares to break his fast. "He's not a bad sort, though my mead is better."

Siebold glared at the man, his lip curling further. His teeth flashed and he gave a deep growl.

I flung myself to my knees, my arm locking around Siebold's neck. "No. You can't. You must hush."

The growl continued. I grabbed the wolf's snout and jerked him to face me. "Listen to me," I snarled, letting my power out. My hair covering slipped and my hair escaped, the tight curls bouncing out.

The wolf glared at me but the growling stopped.

"This is where I've made my home. These are innocent people. They have done nothing to hurt me." *Yet.* "You will not growl at them. You will not attack. And you will not let yourself be seen." I released his maw and wiped my hand on my skirts before hoisting up my basket. "Now stay here and keep out of sight. I'll be back by dusk."

I strode on, without looking to see if the wolf obeyed.

My heart pounded as I entered the market. My path took me past the mead maker. Any moment he might look up. Would he see an ordinary woman? Or would he instantly recognize me as a witch?

My hair cloth had slipped. With a hiss, I tugged it back into place, just in time for Cynog to glance up.

He gave me a polite smile. "Mornin', Mistress Meadhan."

"Master Cynog," I murmured and inclined my head. "Looks to be a fine day."

"A fine day," he agreed, lifting his mug of mead in a happy toast. The tight fist inside me relaxed.

Perhaps everything would be all right.

Then Cynog looked past me and his eyes bulged out of his head. His white skin paled further. "What is that?" he sputtered. The mug of mead dropped to the ground.

I whirled. Siebold was following me. A huge wolf, trotting at my heels through the marketplace.

So much for trying to look ordinary.

"Oh, him?" I squeaked and waved a nervous hand. "He's fine."

"It's a wolf!" Cynog backed up into his stall, no doubt looking for a weapon.

"Wolf hound," I blurted, "And he's harmless."

"Harmless!"

"Well..." I glanced to Siebold. The wolf was grinning, its teeth on full display. "Not harmless. But he won't harm you."

A flurry of shocked voices rose up behind me. More villagers had seen Siebold.

Cynog waved a long knife. "Don't make any sudden moves. I'll distract him and then we must run."

"I'm fine. He's not dangerous. Not to me. See?" I dropped my basket and held out my hand. "Siebold, come."

There was a tense pause where everyone watching held their breath. Then Siebold swung his great head my way, took a step, and let me run my hand over his head.

Cynog visibly wilted with relief. "He's not attacking."

"Of course not." I stepped closer and ran both hands over Siebold's body.

"God's thumbs," Cynog muttered, drawing an arm over his brow. He went to pick up his mug of mead and Siebold swung his head around and fixed the poor man with a baleful stare. Cynog froze.

"Siebold, no," I snapped, tugging the wolf's head back to face me. "Bad dog."

The villagers murmured to one another, watching closely, though none made a move to come closer.

"Mistress Meadhan," Dafydd darted between the staring villagers and ran up, skidding to a halt. "Oh. You brung the wolf?"

"Hound," I corrected desperately. "Wolf hound. He's perfectly trained," I announced to the wary villagers listening. "Really."

"He is that," Dafydd announced. "He does tricks."

"Yes," I cried. "I'll show you. Siebold...sit."

Teeth still bared, the great wolf dropped his haunches.

"Stay." I breathed in relief, moving closer with my hand out. "Down. That's it," I tried not to sound too shocked when Siebold lowered his body to the ground. "Now...roll over."

The wolf's ears twitched but he didn't move.

"He's still learning that one," I said. A few people chuckled.

"'E's a good un," Dafydd crept up and dropped to his haunches. He extended a grubby hand for the wolf to sniff.

We all waited, wide-eyed, to see what the wolf would do.

Siebold sniffed the boy's hand. He ducked his head and bucked at the hand, forcing the boy to pet him.

Relieved murmurs ran through the crowd.

"He's a big un," Cynog commented. "But I suppose that's good for you. Woman living alone out in them woods. Can't be too careful."

"Yes. Too right." I stiffened my knees so I wouldn't sink to the ground in relief.

Dafydd kept petting Siebold, the villagers relaxed and started to drift away. Quickly as that, they seemed to accept the wolf in their midst.

"Mistress Meadhan," someone called. It was Alwyn. Mistress Donna's son came ambling through the throngs. "Good morning." He would've walked right up to my side, but suddenly Siebold was on his feet. Alwyn stopped in his tracks, hand on his long knife as the huge wolf snarled at him.

"Siebold, no," I shouted.

Teeth still bared, Siebold settled back down.

Alwyn's shoulders lowered, though he didn't take his hand from his knife. "I see you still have the wolf."

"Yes," I smiled weakly.

"Shall I walk you to your stall?" he held out a hand for my basket, but Siebold pushed between us.

"I've got it," I fisted my hand in Siebold's ruff just in case he decided to lunge for Alwyn. "It's all right. He's...overprotective."

"Indeed." Alwyn did not hold the wolf's behavior

against me. He chatted amiably as he walked me to my stall, and bowed his head to me before he left, promising to convey my greetings to his mother.

"He does not lack bravery," I muttered to myself as I watched his tall form stride away.

At my side, the wolf growled.

"As for you," I rounded on the wolf. "I expect better behavior from you. Do not growl at my friends."

Friend? Siebold's voice spoke in my head.

"That's right. He's a good man."

In answer, the wolf cocked a leg and let loose a spray of urine in the direction of the retreating man.

"Bad dog," I scolded. The wolf's ears went flat. He didn't like being called a dog, but I'd had enough. "You heard me. Go lie down."

"C'mon, wolfie," Dafydd settled himself near my stall. Siebold trotted over to him. It seemed the two would be my guardians today. I kept an eye on them, but they seemed to get along fine. The wolf never snarled or bit at Dafydd, and the boy was perfectly at ease with the wild creature, being half feral himself.

It took the villagers longer to be brave enough to approach my stall, but by midday I was doing steady business. Siebold mostly bared his teeth at the men, but most of my customers were women. When I noticed a nervous man hanging about, waiting for a chance to slip past the wolf, I gave Dafydd a coin to buy some meat pies and sent the wolf with him. My male customer got his potion before the wolf and boy returned, sharing a pie between them.

"'E likes pies," Dafydd informed me solemnly as the wolf lapped at his fingers.

"He'll eat anything." I shook my head, but watching the wolf befriend the boy made my heart sigh.

"Did you eat all that buck?" Dafydd asked.

"Of course not. There's still plenty. I salted some of it, and put the rest in the smokehouse."

The boy's eyes glittered as I described the food. "You're welcome to come back with us, Dafydd. We'll give you all the meat you can eat, whenever you wish."

Dafydd squinted at me. "You'll make me wash again, though."

"Oh yes." I turned to hide my smile. I noticed the boy's face was cleaner than usual.

"Suppose that's fair," Dafydd shrugged, and went to crouch near the wolf.

Throughout the afternoon, the wolf and boy played in the shadows. As the sun began to dip lower and make way for the moon, a foul shadow came over the market.

"Boy, come away from that creature."

Dafydd stiffened at his father's words.

With the two males standing in the same area, I saw the resemblance. They shared the same beaked nose.

The priest went to cuff the boy. Dafydd cringed. A flash of fur, and Siebold was between them, snarling.

The priest staggered back with a yelp. "He bit me!"

I hurried out from behind my stall. "You should not antagonize him," I said calmly to hide my pounding heart.

The bite was only a scrap of skin on the backside of the priest's hand. Punishment for trying to cuff Dafydd. But the blow had been dealt. A crowd was gathering. And the priest knew he had an audience.

"Behold what evil stirs in the heart of this valley," said the priest.

All eyes went to Siebold who still bared his teeth.

"Siebold," I whispered, but it was too late.

The priest paraded himself in front of our stall,

pandering to the growing crowd. "This is why we need the protection of Offa's men. They will save us."

"Save us from what?" Gruffudd, the blacksmith, called. His daughter Eira, stood beside him, wide eyed.

"From evil." The priest's face turned red. "Witches and demons live in these woods."

A few frowns, but no one disagreed. And in my mind's eye, I saw the flames rise.

This was how it started.

20

S *iebold*

THE TASTE of the male's blood on my tongue was as vile as his stench. I knew the taste of evil. It ran all through this man's veins.

It didn't take my keen eyesight to see that the boy and the foul man were related, though the boy was thin from malnourishment. There was light in Dafydd's eyes where his father's gaze was little more than a dark pit.

As the priest pointed his grubby finger at me, Dafydd edged closer to me. In the distance I saw the men who had tried to take Meadhan. It was time to enact my plan. I would kill those men. Added to the list would be the priest.

But I felt Meadhan's hand at the back of my neck.

Please, she begged.

I heard her words, but it was the vision in her mind that stayed me.

Meadhan, younger, her face round and filled with fear. She crouched in the dark.

Hiding.

Her gaze was latched on a woman.

The woman was older. She had Meadhan's face, but her skin was pale. Her lips were pressed closed. Only to wrench open wide. A howl of pain erupted from her.

In my mind, I could hear Meadhan screaming in terror. But her lips stayed shut. She stayed quiet.

Hiding.

Alone, in the dark, while her mother screamed.

I staggered out of the memory. With a glance at Meadhan, I saw that she'd carefully packed away her thoughts of the past. Her face a mask that no one in this village had ever penetrated. I doubt anyone had ever tried.

I will break all of her defenses. Smash them until she reveals her true nature to me. Only me.

I stood guard as she packed her things from her stall. The priest kept droning on. But no one stopped us from leaving the village and making our way into the forest.

21

M eadhan

I'D SPENT my life in hiding. A few days and this man, this beast, destroyed everything I'd worked for. Everything I'd built.

Siebold shifted in the middle of the forest. I wanted to shout at him even then as the magic shook the leaves free of their branches. He planted himself before me on two legs instead of four. Gloriously naked.

"What were you thinking?" I demanded, keeping my gaze off his ever ready manhood.

"Those men are weaklings." He wiped the comment away as though it were a fly nagging him. "The thugs, the priest. I could dispense of them with a flick of my wrist. And then we could rule this village. Together."

He reached for me. I moved out of his way.

"You saw a handful of men," I said. "But Offa the Bloody

has many men. A pack. You have no idea what a pack can do."

"You would be surprised," he muttered.

"And you were about to attack the priest. Do you know what an important man he is in the village?"

"He hit the boy," Siebold growled.

I looked away at that. I had had the same instinct. But violence was a part of this world. "There are worse things than being hit."

My mother's face flashed in my mind. The bonfire flames rising higher and higher. The echoes of men's voices as they laughed and shouted, *Kill the witch!*

"At least I didn't eat him," Siebold grumbled.

"Is that your excuse? You deserve a treat because you didn't eat someone?"

Siebold shrugged, confusion marring his brow. I would be struck by how beautiful he was if I didn't feel the danger trickling down my spine. The magic in my fingers strained to be released. I balled my hands into fists to keep it contained.

He took me by my shoulders. The magic surged, responding to his touch. It truly was him. He was the cause of my lessening control over what was inside of me. Every time he touched me, the bright sparks in me that I fought so hard to hide would ignite and push against my flesh to be free.

"You need to go," I said, shrugging off his touch.

"Fine, we'll go home."

"No," I whirled on him. "I'm going to my home. You're going wherever you came from."

"I'm not leaving you. You are mine."

"I belong to no man."

His teeth glistened. I knew for certain he wanted to bite

me then, to mark me so that all the world would see that my heart and soul belonged to him. Wolves only mated to those who had magic. If he marked me everyone would know that there was magic inside me.

But it was already too late.

My thoughts turned dark as we reached my home. Siebold had fixed the roof as promised. I'd swept up the pottery, all signs of our violent lovemaking gone. The space felt different. More of a home. I'd made memories here, memories I didn't want to forget. People I didn't want to leave behind.

But I had other, darker memories. And they told me I could not stay.

Siebold watched me pace back and forth.

"Meadhan," he murmured. "Look at me." I refused to do so and he pressed his forehead against mine. Despite myself, my fingers curled in his hair. "It will be alright." His lips found my ear. "I will fix it."

"How?" My voice was broken.

"I will kill them all."

My laugh was half incredulous, half despairing. "You cannot kill them all."

"Then punish them. They cannot be allowed to hurt you."

"I can take care of myself, wolf." I pushed away from him, noting how he stiffened as I turned my back to him.

"Then why have you not done so?" His voice was deep, cold.

I whirled around. "You want me to reveal my powers? Produce some display meant to intimidate them all so they fear me?"

"Yes!"

"I'd be just like Offa and all the rest. The bullies who use fear to rule." My lip curled. "You want that, Siebold? You want me to rule?"

"Why not?" He cocked his head. "You'd be different."

"I cannot do it. I will not use my powers."

"Why not?"

"Because I cannot let them see!" I threw my hands up.

A gust of wind hit the hut and banged the door open. Siebold caught it before it could slam. He latched it firmly and leaned against it for good measure. His posture was calm but his eyes were bright gold.

I didn't care. I started to pace in the tiny space. "You think I like hiding out here? Slinking into the market, healing in secret? Never to use my true powers, never to reveal who I am?"

Siebold's bright eyes followed me back and forth.

"I can't be who I really am. Not now, not ever." I stopped and covered my face with my hands. The vision of my mother's agonized face came unbidden.

Strong hands caught mine. Siebold tangled his fingers with mine. He turned my hand over and kissed the knuckles. "Tell me. Tell me everything."

So I did. "My mother was a witch, with curling red hair and pale skin. My father was a warrior from a faraway land. From him, I got my dark skin. From my mother, my wild hair and magic.

"My father died when I was young. My mother and I traveled for a while. She taught me all I know of herbal lore. And a few spells. We settled in a village, much like this one, but on the outskirts. We had to hide." People feared what they didn't understand. First they might respect it, but respect easily turned to resentment, and resentment to distrust. And distrust to hate. I learned that lesson from my mother, too.

I swallowed, remembering my mother's face from that night. *Everything will be all right, my little moonbeam.* It was a lie. "The men came at night, led by a priest. They accused her of using magic to heal a woman. They told my mother to confess."

"I used no magic. It was only herbs," my mother had said. But she hid the truth. It wasn't just the herbs. I had said an incantation over those herbs. Otherwise, the woman would've died. The magic in my blood compelled me to heal the sick. My mother had told me to hide, and I disobeyed. And for that she died.

"Kill the witch!" the men had shouted. And the wind had kicked up. My mother stared through the crowd straight into my hiding place. She knew my fear was the source of the oncoming storm. The elements bent to my will when my emotions ran high.

No, Meadhan, my mother spoke to me mind to mind, as she never had before. Her voice was faint, but I heard it. *Run and hide.*

"I have to hide," I repeated, my arms around my body. "They are coming. I have to hide."

"Meadhan," Siebold murmured my name, calling me back. "I am here. No one will hurt you."

"Hold me," I begged, and he did. And after a moment, I drew his head down for a kiss. Another moment, and Siebold growled and swung himself over me. He drew my leg up over his hips and entered me even as our lips still sought each other, our tongues tangling. I opened myself and welcomed him into my body.

I could not have a life here, or a home, but I could have this.

22

S *iebold*

SHE WAS PLIANT BENEATH ME. Sedated with my lovemaking, because that was what it was. Not only had I worshiped this witch with my body, I'd poured my heart and soul into her.

I now understood why males would fight to the death for their women, their mates.

Meadhan and I laid in the hut, bare to the midnight moon from the window. I'd brought her to climax after climax. Now she clung to me. And I to her.

Her pulse pounded against my cheek. I turned my face, my nose met with the perfect skin of her neck. It beckoned to me.

My fangs lengthened. My mouth watering to have more of her, all of her. Her dark eyes flashed at me in the moonlight. I held my breath with great difficulty. This was going to happen. She would wear my mark. The question was, would I need to hold her down to give it to her? Or would she accept my claim without a fight?

"Siebold, please. Please, don't stop. Take me. I am yours."

She gave a long sigh. Her eyelids fluttered closed. She turned her face to the side... exposing her neck.

A good man would ask if she was sure. A good man would be gentle.

I was not a good man. I was a beast. And Meadhan belonged to me.

I sunk my teeth deep into her flesh. She screamed, her body convulsing in my arms, her inner muscles squeezing me until I roared and thrust deep. My cock jerked and I spilled my seed.

"Siebold," Meadhan sighed and slumped, spent. Her shoulders jerked once when I licked the mark I'd made, but her eyes remained closed. I waited until the tears in her flesh started to close.

It was done. My bite would heal, but the mark would remain, branding her as mine.

I cradled her close. My eyes grew heavy but I fought sleep, wanting to stay awake a moment longer. Just to be with Meadhan. Just to hold her. For the first time in a century, I was at peace. I held my mate in my arms and now my beast could sleep.

23

M *eadhan*

IT WAS the magic that woke me, not the rays of the sun. The tendrils of light danced over my skin. The warmth touched my eyelids. Heated my lips. A large body stole between my legs and thrusted inside of me.

Siebold.

After bringing me to untold heights into the deepest dark of the night, he demanded more of my body at first light. He found no more resistance within me. I opened to him completely, allowing my desire to flow out of me and join his.

His golden strands were damp on his forehead as he hovered over me. The tawny gold on his chest glistened as he brushed my nipples. I caught glimpses of the thatch between his legs as his curls mingled with my own, slickening us both with our shared passion.

When the act was done, I lay in a stupor. Too tired to move. Still not understanding the spell his body had cast on me. But I knew this could not last. I had to rise. There was still the matter of my livelihood.

Before my feet touched the floor, his large hand snaked out and grabbed me.

"Where do you think you're going?" His voice was more growl than man.

When I looked over at him, his sun gold gaze sparkled with untapped heat. Could he possibly want more? Could I possibly resist?

"I must get to work," I said.

"I'll put you to work," he purred, pulling me to him.

"Life is not all pleasure all day." But my protest was weak as he traced the line between my breasts.

"It will be for you."

"Siebold, please," I giggled at his tickling fingers, then firmed my tone. "I must put food on the table or starve."

"Woman, I brought you food," he said as he nipped at my belly. "If you require more, I'll go out and hunt again. After another a taste of you."

His head dipped lower and I almost gave up fighting. But my body was sore from our lovemaking. My neck throbbed as if it'd knotted up while I slept.

The rest of my body ached, especially between my thighs, but it was a good ache. It felt right.

The warrior's beard brushed my inner thighs and my cunt clenched even as I protested, "Siebold, no. I must rise."

"Why?"

"People expect their herbs and remedies," I explained. "They depend on me."

Siebold lifted his head and frowned. "After the way they treated you? You are not going back to that village."

His edict got my hackles up. In all my life, no one had tried to command me, save my mother. "Think you my lord and husband now? I gave you no vow."

Siebold's grin was wicked and confident. "Yes, you did make a vow. It was when you screamed my name and begged me to take you, to claim you as my own." His gaze dipped to my neck.

Had I said that in the throes of passion? The sound of my hoarse vows, creaking from my cries of passion at this man's hands, blared in my mind. I did say those words. But I did not mean what he thought I meant.

I felt the dread creeping over me. I had hoped I'd imagined it. That it had only been a fevered dream in all the ecstasy.

I remember my pleasure had begun and then his kiss at my neck. When his lips had pressed into my flesh, my pleasure had spiked anew. But it wasn't a heated kiss. His fangs had pierced my skin.

My fingers traced my neck. The raised skin of the mark was plain. All would see it.

"You bit me," I choked out.

"I did." He was still grinning. He didn't understand what he had done.

"You marked me." Marked me as his. Marked me as a witch.

I could no longer hide.

"Why would you do this?"

Siebold's gaze turned serious. "You soothe the beast in me. He wants you for his own."

"I belong to no man."

"I'm not a man. And you're no ordinary woman. Show me your power."

"No."

"Why do you deny this beautiful part of yourself? You were made for me, and I for you."

"No," I insisted, wrenching away from him.

Siebold snarled. "You are mine, Meadhan. Forever."

"I am no man's," I spat, shaking. "Least of all yours. Never yours."

A flash of hurt crossed his face before his expression turned grim. I didn't care.

"Get out," I snapped, and shouted when he did not move. "Out!" I jabbed my finger towards the door.

"Meadhan," he moved towards me. I didn't think. I didn't speak. I raised my hands and my power was there. It blasted him across the room. The door flew open but he fought, grabbing the frame.

"Out," I roared into the rising storm. A great wind rose up like a giant hand and wrenched him from the hut, tossing him into the forest. I stomped after him, arms outstretched as if pushing him away. The trees shivered and shook in the rising storm.

Meadhan, Siebold's voice in my mind was faint.

Out! With a huge blast of power, I forced him from my mind. Clouds covered the sun and a fierce wind whipped at my skirts. I stumbled. My hands hit the dirt and I retched as my power took hold, scouring my insides. The world seemed to rage with my anger until I felt hollow inside.

When I rose, my head ached. Wetness trickled from my ear. I touched it and my fingers came away red. Blood. But my mind was empty and so was my garden and the forest before me.

Siebold was gone.

24

S *iebold*

I RAN THROUGH THE FOREST, blind, my legs pumping and my feet striking the ground. Branches whipped my body and I welcomed the pain. Each step took me away from Meadhan. The beast howled and howled in my mind.

She'd taken me in. I'd held my mate in my arms. But now she cast me out. And I would be forever alone.

I'd rather die than lie with you. Another woman, long ago. Laughing, pushing me away. *I'd rather die.*

I scratched my face, drawing blood. The memories came too fast. The woman laughing, leaving me for another. The beast taking over. My mind consumed. The violent buzzing, like a hive in my skull.

I didn't want to remember. But I couldn't stop myself.

I'd rather die than lie with you, the woman in my memories said. And everything went black. And when I woke, her blood stained my hands.

I'd rather die, she'd said. And she did. I killed her. My beast took over, and when I woke she was dead.

I would always be alone.

Get out! The woman became Meadhan. My mate, my own. She cast me out. Just like my Alphas. Just like my pack.

Get out, Samuel had said. *You are no longer welcome here.* The pack had converged on me, wolves and warriors, warriors and wolves. Ready to rip into me, drive me out.

I would always be alone.

My paws ripped at my face. I was a wolf, and not a wolf. A monster. I threw back my head and howled.

The Change had come and I would never be the same.

25

M eadhan

A HOWL ECHOED in the forest and I shivered. The storm had died but the clouds had not left the sky. I felt cold, but not only because the sun had not come out.

Siebold was gone. I'd cast him out. Just like his pack had.

"Good riddance," I muttered and stomped back into my hut, ignoring the nice new roof the warrior had built.

The mark on my neck throbbed and I covered it with a hand. He marked me without my permission. He deserved my wrath. I was right to cast him out; I should have never let him in.

But instead of angry, I only felt sad.

I puttered around my hut, tidying away bundles of herbs, building a fitful fire. But Siebold was in my every waking thought. In my blood. His bite mark pulsed on my skin.

Should I stay or should I go? I leaned over a water barrel to study the mark at the junction of my neck and shoulder. Perhaps there was a way I could cover it up. Continue to hide.

But when I looked into the smooth surface of the water, it rippled and called my Sight. I Saw a blond wolf, running through the forest. Siebold. He was stumbling and blood trickled down his snout.

With a cry, I dashed a hand into the water, sullying the vision. I could close my eyes but red pain spread through me with every beat of my heart.

Power rippled through me, rising against the pain. It burrowed into my head, taking over. I fell to my knees, temples throbbing. I was in the grip of my Sight and nothing could stop it. I opened my eyes and Saw what it wanted me to see.

Not a vision. A memory.

I ran through the forest, briars scratching my face. Torches blazed ahead.

I flung myself to my belly and crawled through the thicket until I could see.

The men had come again. This time there were more of them. They dragged my mother to the rocky edge of a lake. She stood on the beach, bound, calm amid the violent mob. She was so small and frail beside the angry men. Her pale cheek was bruised where they'd struck her.

Some men stood with torches. Some passed around jugs of mead. Others argued loudly the best way to kill a witch. "Drown her," one said, pointing to the lake.

"No, use an axe." A man sharpened his blade with a whetstone.

But several men raced to the forest where they put axe to

trunk and brought more trees crashing down. They were building a bonfire.

"Kill the witch," they chanted. A priest stood to the side, praying loudly and urging the men to build the bonfire higher.

The power welled up in me. Light rippled along my skin. My hair crackled and rose off my back and neck.

"Meadhan, no!" my mother held out her hand. She looked straight at me, past the mob, past the trees where I hid. My skin prickled under her Sight. "Do not show yourself."

Mother. My lips moved but the sound caught in my throat.

"I am lost. Do not try to save me."

A man touched a torch to the foot of the pyre and a line of flame licked up the side. Cheers echoed over the lake. A man splashed the content of a jug onto the wood and the fire roared in response.

"Kill the witch! Kill the witch!"

I could not see or hear my mother. But her voice spoke faintly into my mind. Run, my moonbeam. Run and hide.

I stayed in the forest, sheltered by the briars, my hands fisted at my sides. As the bonfire flames grew brighter, my power grew weaker and weaker. Trickling out of me. My legs gave out and I slumped on the forest floor.

It wasn't until dawn that I found the strength to rise and slip away from the clearing and the evidence of horrible things all the men had done. I wandered through the woods for days, drinking from streams and eating nothing. Eventually I foraged and found the path that would take me over the mountains, far from the valley where my mother and I had lived.

I would obey my mother's wishes and survive. Instead of using my power, I would hide. This was the final lesson she taught me and I learned it well. I kept my life, but I'd paid a terrible price.

Instead of saving my mother, I watched her die.

26

S *iebold*

THE CURSE WAS UPON ME. In the distance, a swarm of flies was rising, filling the world with their buzzing. I could run forever and not outrun the evil within.

My hands tore at my chest, but they were not hands. They were giant paws. Clawed monstrosities fit for the monster I was. My claws ripped my own flesh but the magic healed me just as quickly. I could not even tear my own heart out. I raised my head to the rising moon and howled.

A shout ahead warned me I was not alone. Men were in the forest with clanking weapons and torches. Hunting.

I stood tall and waited. The first ranks who found me recoiled in terror, but their shouts drew the rest.

"There it is. Kill the beast," they shouted.

I opened my arms and let them come.

I could not kill myself, but I'd let them try. I'd lost Meadhan, my own, and my reason to live was gone.

27

M*eadhan*

THE MEMORY of my mother's death left my heart cracked open. I dragged myself to the water bucket and splashed the cool liquid onto my face. I averted my gaze before another vision took me, and guilt burned in my breast.

I owed it to Siebold, to See him one last time. To bid him goodbye before I packed up and fled like the coward I was.

The water stirred and offered up a vision. Not of Siebold but of the priest. Father Gerald was surrounded by many men. Armed men who carried torches. The priest was urging them on.

"The net is silver," he said. "It will contain the beast."

First they'd hunt him, then they'd hunt me.

My vision turned and twisted, and I Saw Siebold standing proud. He was a monster, his body huge and twisted. Half man and half wolf. The men shouted when they found him and spread in a circle around him.

I waited holding my breath for Siebold to snap out of his trance and fight. But he didn't move. Not when they threw spears. Not when they rushed forward with torch and axe.

He stayed still and let them come.

Siebold, no! Fight!

Meadhan, his voice came clear into my mind. *My love. My own.* I felt his anguish in the bond.

I'm here. I snatched up my cloak. *I'm coming!*

No! Stay away. Do not come close.

But I could not stay away. They would torture him. He would heal over and over. He would allow them to do this, to protect me.

I could not hide any longer.

I raced down the path, my heart pounding in my breast. The magic pulsed through me, and my feet unerringly knew where to turn. My power was like a compass guiding me.

Run, Meadhan. Run and hide, Siebold's voice blended with my mother's. *Hide what you are and survive.*

"I cannot. I cannot hide any longer." I whispered.

At last I came to the circle of torches. The men whooping and cheering, surrounding the beast. I burst into the clearing before I had a plan.

Before I could think, my hands filled with light. I would not cower from this. These predators would find no prey here.

I had been at sea when a storm struck. I knew what it was like to have the wind and the waves bash against a boat until you think you might die. But now I was the storm. I was the wind and wave. I was the flood.

A great whoosh of power left me. A crack of light split

the clearing and the men fell. People screamed, the wind howled.

But inside me there was peace. My power came when I called and there was so much more, and endless well deep within.

The thugs struggled to rise. I unballed my fists, preparing for the next attack.

The men were down, but they weren't the only ones. Siebold lay on the ground, covered in a net. Bound and bloody with broken spears sprouting from his flesh.

Get up, Siebold. Heal yourself. You can do it.

"It's the witch," someone shouted. "This is her demon creature."

"Kill them both! Kill the witch!"

"No," I cried. I raised my palms to the sky and brought my arms down. Power whooshed out, knocking the thugs down again.

"Leave this place," I ordered. And the thugs scuttled upright and ran. They would tell the village what I was, and they'd come for me. But at least Siebold would be all right.

I threw off the net, cursing when it caught on his wounded limbs, and he bellowed. When he was free, I sank to the ground, reaching for him. He shuddered in the dirt.

His wounds were healing, but his body was grotesque. Twisted. Half man, half wolf. All monster.

"It's my fault," I whispered. "I did this to you." I tentatively touched his paw. His elbows tipped with fur, matted with dirt and blood.

Meadhan. Siebold's voice moved in my mind, an intimate caress. *You should not have come.*

I had fought him speaking straight into my thoughts, but now warmth spread through me at the sound.

"They wanted to kill you. I couldn't let them take you. I couldn't let you die."

He lifted one shoulder. Blood had trickled down his forehead, leaving a rusty trail. His wounds were slowly knitting but he ignored them, cupping my face in his monstrous paws.

"They would've cut off your head," I insisted. "I couldn't let that happen. I've seen it before. I've seen it--" my voice choked off.

"Shhh," Siebold's clawed fingers carefully wiped away my tears. "You stopped them. We are safe now."

He was wrong. We would never be safe again, not until we packed up our lives and fled this valley. I'd done it before. I'd probably have to do it again.

But we were alive. We would survive.

Siebold kept stroking my forehead and cheeks as if reassuring himself I was really in his arms. "You came for me," he murmured. "No one else has done that. No one else thought I was worth saving."

"You are worth it," I told him fiercely.

His mouth tipped downwards, but he didn't contradict me.

"You are mine," I said.

"I am a monster," he said in his deep voice.

I stroked his face and spoke into his mind. *There's a monster that lives inside all men. Only a strong woman can tame it.*

He rolled, taking me with him. His body settled over me. He lowered his head to my neck, licking and grazing the fragile skin with his teeth. *You are my woman.*

I reached down between us and circled his cock with my hand. Siebold growled even as his member throbbed in my palm. *And you are my monster.*

Siebold growled again. Heat broke over me. My cunt gushed with liquid. The warrior worked over me, rubbing his great body against mine, drawing my leg up to hook around his waist even as his hand fisted in my hair. I opened my legs and cried out as he entered me. He was thick and swollen, stretching me to the point of pain. I gasped and hung onto his shoulders. Slowly my body opened, easing his way. Pleasure ran like lightning up my back, weakening my limbs.

Mine. Siebold surged between my legs. The coarse hair on his chest rubbed my soft skin. I twined my legs around his thrusting hips, tugging him closer.

Mine, I answered. I let my head fall back and loosed the power building inside me. Light flashed in the dark forest, rivaling the moon. My eyes and hands were filled with light.

I tugged Siebold's head down and opened my mouth, sealing his lips against mine. I let my will out, let it surge into him. Power poured from my mouth into his until his eyes blazed like the sun. Light spread through his great body, seeking out every dark corner, every bit of rot. Driving out the curse.

I braced myself and rolled, bringing Siebold with me. His massive body lay under mine. I worked over him, my brown hands stark against his tan chest. My hips slapped into his. I fucked him hard. I claimed his body as mine. He belonged to me and I would not tolerate his body, mind, or soul enslaved by a curse any more.

Siebold blinked up at me. I rolled my body over his, stretching upwards, preening as his eyes lit watching my lush curves. His hands found my hips and he thrust upwards. My head shot back, light shooting miles high, a fiery arc. A comet born of our lovemaking. My climax blazing through me, unhinging my spine.

I collapsed and my power caught me. It lifted me and Siebold higher. The ground beneath us burst into flames, not born of flint or tinder, but magic. Phoenix fire, burning the world clean. Destroying the old, making life anew.

As we rode the air over a circle of flame, Siebold grabbed me. His claws ghosted over my skin, but did not slice me. I grasped him, pulling him closer. My thighs were slick with our lovemaking. My cunt gripped Siebold's cock tight until he roared his own pleasure into the night.

I WOKE with a stick digging into my side. I rolled to my feet and turned in a circle. Here and there, a few final embers glowed. The wind caught the grey remnants of ash and carried them away.

My power had lowered us gently to the ground.

There were leaves and twigs in my hair. My hands shook. I held them in front of me and marveled. My dark skin was tinged with gold.

I felt hollowed out, scoured clean as a vessel of magic. But when I looked inside, my power was there. An endless well. It would always be there, ready to come when I called.

In the center of the circle, a man lay on the burned ground. His hair and beard were a bit singed but he was a man. All man. All mine. My Siebold.

He opened his eyes and smiled. He opened his arms and I went to him, draping myself over him. My head tucked under his chin, fitting perfectly. Siebold lifted a hand to stroke my hair and I let him.

"You're back," I murmured. He was a man again. I sensed his monstrous form deep inside, but it was calm. Quiet. A predator well-fed and sated.

"Yes. The beast sleeps." He shifted me in his arms and pulled a singed leaf from my hair, crumpling it in his palm before letting the wind blow the pieces away.

After a while he said, "You lied to me."

I raised my head. He greeted me with a lazy smile. "You told me you couldn't tame a wild wolf."

I chuckled and lay back down, resting my head in the hollow of his chest where his coarse blond hair tickled my cheek. His heart beat strong and steady under my ear. "I didn't tame the wolf. I simply loved him."

28

S *iebold*

MEADHAN AND I laid in the forest, bare to the midnight moon. I'd brought her to climax after climax. Now she clung to me. And I to her.

Her pulse pounded against my cheek. I turned my face, my nose met with the perfect skin of her neck. It beckoned to me.

My fangs lengthened, my mouth watering to have more of her, all of her. Her dark eyes flashed at me in the moon-light. I held my breath with great difficulty.

I had already marked her. But I needed to do it again. And likely again after that. The question was would I need to hold her down to give it to her? Or would she accept my claim without a fight?

She gave a long sigh. Her eyelids fluttered closed. She turned her face to the side... exposing her neck.

A good man would ask if she was sure. A good man would be gentle.

Meadhan's gaze flicked open for a second. Her brow quirked as though she knew what I was thinking. Her lip curled. She knew exactly what and who I was.

I was not a good man. I was a beast. A beast she accepted as her own.

I asked nothing. My bite struck hard. She cried out in a scream of agony that ended in the deepest pleasure. And then she was wholly mine.

29

M *eadhan*

DAWN CREPT UP ON US, filling the forest with reddish light. Siebold and I rose and walked slowly back to my hut, hand in hand.

His bite burned my flesh, searing his mark into me forever. I could no longer hide what I was, who I was. I was a witch, a being of great power, and I belonged to the beast.

We reached my garden and I quickened my steps. "I will pack. We need to go."

Siebold didn't ask me why. He knew as well as I that Offa's men would return in greater numbers. Silently he helped me roll my quilts and wrap up the vials filled with my best herbal remedies so they could be easily carried.

I watched him out of the corner of my eye as he moved with fluid grace beside me. His body was no longer monstrous, but that of a well-formed man. He looked at home in my hut, but it struck me odd that such a beautiful man wanted to belong to me.

I swallowed several times, staring at the hearth as I asked, "You will come with me?"

Instantly Siebold dropped the jug he was wrapping and pulled me into his arms. My palms rested on his chest, my fingers threading through the coarse golden hair.

"You are mine, Meadhan," he dipped his forehead to touch mine. "And I am yours. Wherever you go I will be by your side."

Close as we were, his hard cock pressed into my leg. It distracted me. My honeyed scent swirled around us, making Siebold's eyes flare gold.

I opened my mouth to speak--and heard the crash of the garden gate. Siebold was out the door in an instant, with me not far behind.

"Siebold, no, it's Dafydd!"

Siebold had the boy by the scruff of the neck, holding him aloft like a recalcitrant kitten.

"Mistress Meadhan," the boy exclaimed, staring into the warrior's golden eyes.

"It's all right," I hastened to Siebold's side. "He won't hurt you. Siebold." I laid my hand on the warrior's rigid arm. "Siebold, let him down."

Siebold lowered the boy to the ground but kept himself between me and the boy.

He's a child, I said to Siebold.

Children see more than we want them to see, Siebold warned, even as the boy spoke up.

"'E's the wolf?" Dafydd asked.

I sighed. No use denying it any longer. "Yes."

"'E's the monster they're talking about, then." The boy squinted at Siebold.

Siebold and I exchanged a look.

Dafydd glanced around, taking in my pack and rolled quilt. "You're leaving?"

"Yes," I started to explain but the boy burst out.

"You can't! Offa's come. 'E's at the village now."

"That is why we must go."

"They hurt Mistress Donna," Dafydd burst out.

I froze. "What?"

"They took her sons. Said they must help fight the witch and demon beast." Dafydd looked up at Siebold and sniffed. "Demon beast. That's you."

"Dafydd," I leaned down to the boy's eye level. "Tell me what happened." Up close I could tell the boy had bruises under the dirt on his face, but whether they were old or new I couldn't tell.

"She sent me to warn you," Dafydd said.

"Mistress Donna?"

"They came to her house. Pounded on the door and asked for her sons. Any able bodied man," he pronounced carefully as if repeating the summons. "She told them off, she did. That's when they hit her."

I sucked in a breath, my stomach flipping. Short and pale skinned, Mistress Donna reminded me of my mother.

"Go on," Siebold ordered Dafydd, even as he put his hand on my arm to steady me.

"They hit her and she fell. That's when her sons came out. They fought Offa's men but there were too many. They drug them away. But they didn't notice me," he announced proudly. "I helped Mistress Donna up. She said to run and get you."

"They's gathering all the men. Said they'll make an army. The blacksmith wouldn't come, but they took his daughter and set fire to his forge. So he went too. I'm too little, they don't want me." He wiped his nose, signaling an end to his narrative.

I stood frozen. *What do we do? Do we go or do we run?*

Siebold's hand cupped my elbow. He dipped his head to my ear. "We should go. We can take the boy."

"I can't leave," I whispered. Then, louder, "I won't leave."

Siebold's eyes blazed, but he didn't say anything for a long moment. He cocked his head to the side, studying me. "You would risk your life for these villagers?"

Just like that, I was decided. "I'm the only one who can save them." I put a hand to Siebold's cheek. "Will you help me?"

He tilted his head, pressing into my palm. "I told you before. Where you go, I go. I will always be by your side."

I held his face a moment before turning to Dafydd. "Where is Offa? Can you show me?"

The boy gulped and nodded.

I grabbed a cloak and shrugged into it. I already wore my boots and a traveling gown. Siebold strapped a knife to his thigh and shouldered an axe.

"Let us go," I ordered. The three of us set off into the forest.

The time for hiding was over.

30

S *iebold*

THE BOY LED us down the forest path to the place of the market. Before we could break from the forest, I held out my hand, forcing both Meadhan and Dafydd to stop.

"Wait here," I told them, and Changed into the wolf. The boy gasped but I ignored it. I lowered my head and followed the stench of strange men to the flower filled meadow where Meadhan had once had a stall.

The clearing was transformed. Gone were the stalls, destroyed and broken apart to feed a massive bonfire. An army of men trampled the flowers, laying waste to the meadow. Under their boots it'd become a morass of piss and mud.

The field reeked of violence and anger. Every man held a weapon and stank of bloodlust.

I looked my fill and loped back the way I came.

"They've taken over the market area," I told Meadhan after I Changed back. The boy stared as I retied my leather loincloth and refastened my long knife to my thigh before picking up my axe.

"How many?" Meadhan asked. Her face was calm, but I knew she trembled under her cloak.

"Five score," I shrugged. "Perhaps more."

"You going to fight them?" Dafydd asked me eagerly.

I tilted my head and smiled. "If my lady so wishes."

Meadhan snorted. "You're not in armor."

"Don't need armor," I told him. "I'm a Berserker."

Dafydd wrinkled his nose, thinking this over.

"Dafydd," Meadhan interrupted. "I need you to run and get Mistress Donna. Make sure the men don't see you, but rescue her and hide her away. Can you do that?"

A nod.

"Good lad," I handed him my long knife. "Be safe."

The boy looked delighted by my knife, but Meadhan pressed her lips together, her face troubled as she watched Dafydd go.

Once he was gone, she whirled on me. "He's just a boy."

"He's the same age you were when you watched your mother die," I said, and caught her in my arms when she wilted. "Forgive me, Meadhan."

"No," she whispered. "It's true. Dafydd is brave. He is willing to rush into danger. He should be armed."

"He will be all right."

"Only if we stop Offa." She turned her head towards the field. Smoke rose, tinging the sky with grey.

I held my woman's small body against mine, feeling her shake. She was afraid.

"We don't have to do this," I said. "You don't have to face them."

She raised her face to mine. "Yes, I do." She pulled away, tugging at her cloak. "I must."

I caught her chin in my fingers. "I will be by your side. You are not alone."

"I know." She blew out a breath. "It will end now. One way or another, it ends."

31

M eadhan

I STRODE to the edge of the forest and my feet faltered. The field was full of men. As Siebold reported, they'd torn down the stalls and used the scraps to erect a platform erected for their leader. Offa the Bloody was short and squat and grizzled. But he had an air about him that made men follow the orders he barked from his dais. Beside him stood Father Gerald. The priest was clad in his long robes, hands folded piously before his rotund stomach.

The rest of the men milled around. Some were drinking. Others laughed and talked, honing their weapons. Others went to and fro, obeying Offa's bidding. I craned my neck, rising to tiptoe, but then the wind shifted and brought a stench that told me everything.

They were building a bonfire.

I stumbled back, throat raw, eyes watering. *Siebold,* I reached out mentally.

I'm here. The warrior was at my back, steadying me.

Together we slipped around the edge of the field, walking closer to the village. From this vantage point I could see what Offa planned. They'd built the platform between the marketplace and the village. Most of the men waited in the field, but a few gangs had entered the village. The smithy was burning. As I watched, men restrained Gruffudd, the blacksmith, who bellowed and fought. There were too many for him. Offa's men laughed and taunted. Beside the burning building, the cow had been lead out of its pen and butchered. In the pen now were two huddled forms I recognized. Alys and Eira, the young girls I'd often seen at market. They hugged each other, crying, standing in the middle of the pen, their faces averted from the men jeering at them.

A loud voice carried to me on the edge of the field. Cynog stood at the foot of the platform, shouting up at Offa, arguing. To the side, I saw another knot of Offa's mercenaries. These guarded a few more prisoners, men I recognized as villagers. One of them was Alwyn, face bruised and forehead bloody.

It was as Dafydd reported. They'd come for Alwyn. Mistress Donna had protested and they'd struck her down. Alwyn had fought, but they'd taken him, and his brothers, anyway.

As I watched, Cynog found his argument ended when Offa waved a hand. Men dragged Cynog away even as he still protested.

"The time has come. We've gathered here to free this land from evil," the priest announced. "There is wickedness that ferments in this village. You allowed the evil in, but today we will cast it out.

"Bring me the beast. I want its head."

At my side, Siebold growled.

Steady, I ordered. *Hold.*

"The ones to slay it--" Offa pointed to the pen where Alys and Eira huddled together, "will have first pick of the women."

A cheer went up. "Kill the witch! Kill the beast!" Men raised their weapons. They threw their jugs of mead on the fire and whooped as the flames roared higher.

Another bonfire was growing inside me. It spread through my limbs. My spine straightened, my arms stretched out at my sides, palms out. Overhead, a storm was brewing. Thunder rumbled, but the men cheering in the field didn't notice. Soon they would rush the forest to look for monsters.

"Meadhan?" Siebold's voice was thickened. Out of the corner of my eye, I could see his giant, hunched form. Not quite man, not quite beast. He was every bit the monster they would name him.

But he was not a monster anymore. Not to me. The only monsters were here before me, celebrating while the women they would rape later cried in a cattle pen.

Enough was enough.

"Now." I strode from the forest. The wind hit my back. *Not yet,* I whispered to my power. She moved in me, a beast made of light, a golden wolf of my own.

A group of men raised their heads as I passed. A few stared and pointed, but no one came to approach until we were halfway across the field.

"Hey," one shouted. At my side, Siebold snarled.

A murmur moved through the crowd. "It's him! It's the beast!"

On their platform, Offa and the priest snapped their heads in our direction.

I let the hood of my cloak fall back. My hair sprung out, a living thing, a soft brown halo. Men were edging closer, holding weapons. Siebold let loose a growl that shook the earth. The mercenaries shouted, but fell back. Now that they saw him in broad daylight, none were drunk enough to rush the monster.

"Offa, you have laid claim to this valley. None dare stand against you. But I do. I challenge you."

"Who are you?" Offa had drawn his sword. His face was flushed, but he didn't lack bravery.

"I am Mistress Meadhan."

Father Gerald dipped close to Offa, whispering in the leader's ear. Spewing poison, calling me a witch. Offa's eyes narrowed.

"I am here to protect this village," I said. "I will defend it by any means necessary. I'll show you and your men mercy if you leave. Now."

"And if we don't?"

"Then I will show you what I am."

"I know what you are," Offa spat. "A witch woman. Pitiful. Hiding in the forest, luring small children to your home to eat."

Cannibalism? That was new.

"I am here to protect this village," I repeated. "I don't eat children. I am guilty of no crime. But if you do not leave now, you will die."

"Now," Offa shouted, but not to me. His men rushed forward, a wall of would-be rapists, dirty weapons raised high.

Siebold roared and charged into the fray. He was a blond blur, sending his axe spinning through the enemy. Blood sprayed. He fought and fought and fought while I waited and prayed.

For a moment it seemed the battle would be won. I stood untouched in a red circle, the outer rim marked by bodies and torn limbs.

But still the men came. There were so many. For every man that fell, ten more pushed forward to take his place.

On the platform, Offa waved a hand, and a group of men detached. They went to Alwyn and Gruffudd the blacksmith, wrestling them down and putting blades to their throats. More ran to the cattle pen, where Alys and Eira shrieked and clung to each other, crying anew.

"You protect this village?" Offa shouted across the field to me. "Watch them die." He lifted his arm in the air. When it came down, my friends would die.

Siebold bellowed but he was overwhelmed. He could not kill them all. Not quickly enough. If I did not act now, Offa's men would slaughter everyone I knew. Then his men would run into the village and kill everyone they found.

It was time to show them all who I was.

I raised my arms. Lightning crackled to earth and struck my palms. I called the power, and it came. A rushing wave roaring behind me, crashing through the forest, rising as a massive wall, tall enough to cast a shadow over the meadow and blot out the sun.

Men turned up their faces to the darkening sun and cried out.

The power rolled and bounced under me. My feet left the earth. I hung in the air, arms extended. A flick of my fingers, and the men holding Alwyn and Gruffudd fell to the ground, clutching their throats. Another flick and the men around Siebold were blasted backwards.

"You wanted to know what I am? Look to me and behold the truth." My voice was a terrible thing. I shoved the air in front of me and lightning struck the men trying to get to Alys and Eira.

"See me. See me and despair." Wind whipped the earth, dust rising. I pointed to the dais where Offa stood. He and the priest flung himself off the platform a second before it exploded. Father Gerald scrambled to his feet and raced into the village, disappearing.

Offa rose more slowly. He was nothing but a little man on the ground, screaming and ordering his men to fight his battles for him.

"You wanted to kill a witch?" my voice rose as a tornado hit the ground at my feet, flinging mercenaries to either side as it cut a path straight to the bonfire. "Now you will burn." The tornado hit the fire and became the fire, a towering wind tunnel made of debris and flame. Smaller tornados split off and seemed like living things, chasing down mercenaries and burning them alive.

The screams rose from the earth and pleased the monster within me. But Offa was not dead. Not yet.

The whole field rumbled. The earth beneath me cracked. The world split in two, a chasm opening and swallowing men whole. The jagged seam ran straight through the platform debris. It forked and kept going until at last it reached the place where Offa stood. A frightened yelp, a few flailing motions with his sword, and he fell. In an instant, he was gone.

But it was not over. Power crashed through me, filling me to the brim until my eyes shone with a terrible light. A wave of fire hit the village, setting roofs aflame.

Yesssss, something inside me hissed. *Let it all burn.*

"Meadhan," Siebold bellowed over the howling storm. He'd half fallen in the chasm and was hanging from a single paw. I sent a gust of wind to lift him out, and he went tumbling head over heels into the dust. The chasm shuddered and closed.

But the fires still raged. My mother had been murdered, her body mutilated and thrown onto a pyre.

They should pay, a monstrous voice inside me whispered. *They should all pay.*

"Meadhan," Siebold stood on two feet, a monster with a giant's body and wolf's head. *I love you. I love you.*

Something shuddered through me.

I love you. Come, let us build a life together. Come down, and we will build a home.

The monster within me raised her head. Yes, this is what she wanted.

I blinked and woke as if from a dream. I heard the frightened cries of the people below. Villagers running from their homes.

This is not what I wanted.

I threw my arms up. "Let the rain come," I commanded. "Come and heal this land."

Yes, another voice inside me said. My mother's voice. *Well done.*

The air currents under my feet slowly died, lowering me to the ground. I stood with my head uncovered, my face turned up to the wave of rain as it came and snuffed the fires out.

32

S *iebold*

SHE WAS MAGNIFICENT, my Meadhan. I let the rain wash the blood and sweat from my fur, and watched her small form hover aloft in the air. Slowly the power drained from her and lowered her to the ground. I waited until she straightened and then rushed to her side.

The beast within me would not rest until I checked her all over.

"I'm fine," she repeated over and over as my claws stroked over her brow, her cheeks and lips, her arms and sides and all her curves. "I'm fine."

But she stroked my face and fur, checking me over. The rain washed us clean and the storm blew away, leaving us blinking in the sun.

I brushed water droplets from her brow, noting the golden shimmer. *Meadhan, you're glowing.*

She flushed. "I can't help it. It will fade."

She seemed embarrassed, so I merely nodded. I didn't tell her the truth: to me, she'd always glowed. From the first, I Saw her light, her true form. I'd always See her. To me, she would always rival the sun.

"You did it." I knelt so our heads would be the same height. I had shrunk a little. With every second that passed I looked more like a man. But I was still a monster. Meadhan's monster.

"We both did it," she said. She leaned in and clasped me gently until I pulled her close.

"Meadhan, my love, my own." I thought of all that had passed. All the power that had its source in the small woman holding me. I had no words for it. "Are you all right?"

She blinked up at me, then at the village. She stared at the closed rift in the earth where the bonfire had burned. When she looked back up at me, tears tracked down her dark cheeks. "No. But I will heal."

"Come." I gathered her up and set her on her two feet. "Let's go home."

33

M *eadhan*

IF I'D HAD my way, Siebold and I would've slunk off into the forest. But I couldn't leave without checking on the villagers. Few of Offa's mercenaries were left. Fewer still were still whole. Villagers went from body to body, checking to make sure they were all dead.

Alwyn and Cynog straightened as Siebold and I approached.

"You saved us!" Alys cried out. Eira nodded, tears tracking down her face. "Thank you, thank you."

"We owe our lives," Gruffudd said. He knelt, tugging his daughter down with him. The rest of the villagers sank to their knees, until I looked over a sea of kneeling people.

"No, no," I said, spreading my hands. "Do not kneel to me."

The villagers murmured to each other, but started to rise.

"Mistress Meadhan," Mistress Donna called. She emerged from the forest, led by Dafydd. The boy broke from her side and ran to me. I reached down and took his hand.

"Are the bad men gone now?" he asked.

"Yes," I told him. "Forever." I raised my chin and addressed the villagers. "If any of Offa's men survived, send word to me and I will return to this valley." I patted Dafydd's shoulder and started to walk away. Siebold fell into step beside me. Best we left before the villagers decided I was a threat.

But we'd not gone more than a few feet before Mistress Donna cried out, "Wait! Where are you going?"

Something in her tone made me turn. "You do not want me to leave?"

"You destroyed Offa," Cynog pushed closer, stopping short when Siebold growled. "His reign is ended." He spread his hands. "Who will rule this valley, if not you?"

Rule? A lightning bolt fizzed from the crown of my head to the soles of my feet. My hand gripped Siebold's harder.

'Yes," Mistress Donna said, and glanced at her sons. They all were nodding. She cleared her throat and glared at the rest of the villagers.

"Yes," Gruffudd agreed slowly. "Yes."

"No!" The priest cried, shouldering his way through the crowd. "This is her! She is the witch! Kill the witch!"

The villagers all stared at him. None moved.

"Kill her." Sweat ran down the priest's forehead. "Kill her!" He picked up a rock and Siebold started for him.

"No," I grabbed Siebold's arm. Though he was much, much stronger than me, he let me pull him back. He settled himself in front of me, shielding me from the priest.

"People of the village, make your choice," Siebold said. "It's him," he pointed at Father Gerald. "Or us." He waited a long moment, but everyone was silent. He jerked up his chin. "Very well. We will go." He whirled and put an arm around my shoulders, ushering me away.

"No," Gruffudd grunted, and then called louder. "No."

"What do you mean, no?" the priest cried.

"You," Gruffudd pointed at the priest, mimicking Siebold's growl. "Go."

"Yes," Cynog and Alwyn chimed in. "Go."

"Best be on your way now." Mistress Donna folded her arms in front of her. "Before we decide it's a mistake to let you live."

The priest looked from one hard face to another. "You can't mean it."

"Go," Gruffudd reached down and picked up a large rock of his own. "Or we'll make you."

The priest retreated a few shuffling steps. He glanced around, still looking for an opening, a sign of mercy. But there was none.

"Very well," he muttered, and raised his voice in a pious tone. "The Good Lord said if we ever met a place that would not accept the truth, shake the dust off your feet--"

Siebold growled. The sound was loud enough to echo off the mountains. The villagers tensed and the priest scuttled away, but not before noticing Dafydd standing by.

"Boy," the priest snapped his fingers. "Come."

"No," Dafydd said.

"Boy, you will listen to me and come."

Dafydd shrugged and slipped past him.

"Boy! I am your father."

"I have no father. That's what you told me," Dafydd called over his shoulder, and loped the last few feet to me.

"Come," Siebold said. "Let's go home." He tousled Dafydd's hair. "You too, brave warrior."

The boy beamed up at him.

"I'll be by tomorrow," Mistress Donna called.

I was grateful for Siebold's arm around my shoulders

"So, we're not leaving," I said in a daze.

"No," Siebold grinned at Dafydd, who'd run ahead. "But we might need a bigger home."

"We will?"

"For the boy. Don't worry, I will settle him outside tonight."

"What for?" I asked. When I looked at his face, the heat in his eyes made me flush.

"For privacy. I wish to have you to myself tonight." And as arousal surged through me, he dipped his mouth to my ear, nipping lightly then sucking away the hurt before murmuring. "All this fighting makes me want you."

EPILOGUE

M *eadhan*

THE CLANK of steel roused me from my nap. Loud cries drifted in from outside the lodge, along with the whine of weapons, clack of shields, and other sounds of battle.

"Die, wolf spawn!" a high pitched voice shrieked.

"Come take me then, whelp," came a growl.

More banging as the fight commenced.

Then, "No, no. I told you. You cannot hold your shield like that."

"Why not?" Dafydd pitched, his voice matched Siebold's, but it cracked halfway through.

A lower murmur as Siebold explained. Then the mock shouts went up again, as Dafydd tried to attack, and Siebold deflected easily, continuing to lecture in a low voice.

I relaxed against my pillow and smiled. Siebold and

Dafydd sparred every day now. Most of the day, since I was finding it harder and harder to move.

A twinge in my back made me moan. I tried to roll and found my big belly in the way. My arms flailed as I tried to get up.

Meadhan? Siebold's mind touched mine a second before his step sounded in the lodge. He appeared, frowning down at me.

I smiled up at him from my half-propped position. "I cannot get up. I am too large."

"Here, my love." He lifted me easily and carried me to the hearth.

I groaned as I shifted in a new position, rubbing my belly. "This babe will come soon."

"Now?" Siebold asked, his eyes widening slightly with alarm.

"No, not now," I grumbled. "More's the pity."

"Mistress Meadhan?" a woman's voice called. Someone was at the lodge entrance.

A half growl, half sigh rumbled in Siebold's chest. "Why won't they go away?"

I reached up and clasped his hand, threading my small fingers through his long, ones. "It was your idea to build our lodge closer to the village."

"So you wouldn't have to walk too far to market," Siebold defended himself. "Not that you need to walk to market anymore. Everyone comes to you."

"I'm here," I called, and when Siebold scowled, I wagged a finger at him. "Do not growl at my customers."

"They better not take long," he said before rising. He would lurk by my side as I greeted and spoke with our visitors. He kept his arms crossed and glowered at them, especially if they were long in leaving. He did this every time.

I secretly loved it.

Today my visitors were Alwyn and Eira. "Greetings, Mistress," the lovely young woman curtsied. I waved at her so she would stop. Half the village still fell to their knees when I passed. I'd gotten the other half to stop, but the bows and curtsies continued. Siebold had shrugged when I complained of it.

You killed the one who'd rule over them. You're their lord now. It is your due.

"Mistress Donna sends her greetings," Eira said. "She is busy with births in the neighboring village, but she says she will be back for yours."

"Of course. And how are you feeling?" I asked Eira, and she blushed. Her hand rubbed her still flat belly and she glanced up at Alwyn, her new husband.

"The sickness still comes."

I nodded. "It might for a while. You might try these herbs," I shared a packet of my favorite blend, explaining how to brew it.

Eira took it with another curtsey.

"Dafydd has the herbs for your mother," I told Alwyn. "See him before you leave."

"Yes, Mistress," Alwyn said quietly. He held a large cabbage-wrapped bundle in his hands. "Here." He laid his offering on our hearth. "Our thanks." He bowed his head and put his arm around his bride. The new couple left soon after, with Siebold ushering them from my presence.

"I wish they wouldn't do that," I sighed and pointed to the meat when Siebold returned. Since Offa's death, I'd received gifts and offerings. Meat and grain, mostly.

"They pay tribute. They know who saved them."

"I'm not their ruler."

"No?" Siebold shrugged. My skin prickled with magic as he called the Change.

A large blond wolf stood in my lodge, its snout pointed at my hearth.

"Don't you dare," I shouted, but it was too late. The wolf had gulped the meat, cabbage and all.

Cabbage. Blech.

"Serves you right. That was my meat!"

The only meat you eat is mine.

I threw a pillow at him, but the wolf had already trotted away. He disappeared, returning at dusk as a man with a great stag slung over his shoulders.

"We feast tonight," he called to Dafydd, who whooped. Together they loped into the forest to cut down a tree for our fire.

Later that night, the sparks flew to the sky.

"Boy's growing," Siebold said.

"Mmm," I agreed. In the past year, Dafydd had shot up like a weed. Not only that, he'd put on some much needed weight. He looked as healthy as one of Donna's sons, ruddy cheeked. "He'll be a handsome one."

"Handsome?" Siebold raised a blond brow.

I rolled my eyes. "Not as handsome as you."

No one's as handsome as me, Siebold spoke into my mind. Out loud he told a yawning Dafydd to go to bed. The boy obeyed, whining until Siebold promised another day of sparring. Once Dafydd was gone, Siebold turned to me.

He strode my way, his large body fluid and supple, his hair glinting gold in the firelight. He stretched out beside me, twining my fingers with his. I still couldn't believe this warrior was mine.

"Meadhan," he purred. His long fingers danced up my arm. I shifted in my seat.

"Siebold," I couldn't help a little quiver in my voice. The sight of him, the barest touch and I was ready to lie with him again by the fire, under the full moon.

The quirk in the side of his mouth told me he knew the path my thoughts had taken. *We're alone now...*

"Not quite alone," I put a hand on my belly. The little one I carried gave an eager kick.

"Soon, little moonbeam," I crooned to the life inside me. The baby squirmed. "She will be as much trouble as her father, I can already tell."

"She?"

"Aye."

Siebold's eyes glowed with wonder. His fingers shook as his hand came to my belly. His daughter gave a mighty kick where her father touched and I glowed from the inside out.

"Come love me, wolf." I reached for him, and let him ease me over him. As I straddled him, he stroked my arm. If I looked hard enough, I could see the shimmer, faintly luminous in the dark. It was something I could not hide. But with Siebold here, I would never need to hide who or what I was ever again.

Hope you enjoyed this book!
If you want more Berserkers, start with <u>Sold to the Berserkers</u>.

Love, Lee

FREE BOOK

Get two secret Berserker books, Bred by the Berserkers and
A Berserker Birth, available exclusively to you:

A NOTE FROM LEE SAVINO

Hey there. It's me, Lee Savino. I'm so glad you read this book and ordered it directly from my store. Readers like you make my author life possible! And being an author is a dream come true.

If you're like me, you're wondering what to read next. Let me help you out...

If you haven't yet, check out the two exclusive extras I wrote in the Berserker world. They're available here:

Bred by the Berserkers
https://geni.us/BredBerserkerNONL

A Berserker Birth
https://geni.us/BirthBerserkerNONL

And if you want more Berserkers, you can find the complete selection at my store or get the 15 book bundle here!

WANT MORE BERSERKERS?

These fierce warriors will stop at nothing to claim their mates...

Get a 15 e-book Berserker bundle on sale at my Lee Savino shop!

The Berserker Saga

Sold to the Berserkers – Brenna, Samuel & Daegan
Mated to the Berserkers – Brenna, Samuel & Daegan
Bred by the Berserkers (FREE novella only available to you)
– Brenna, Samuel & Daegan
Taken by the Berserkers – Sabine, Ragnvald & Maddox
Given to the Berserkers – Muriel and her mates
Claimed by the Berserkers – Fleur and her mates
Rescued by the Berserker – Hazel & Knut
Captured by the Berserkers – Willow, Leif & Brokk
Kidnapped by the Berserkers – Sage, Thorbjorn & Rolf
Bonded to the Berserkers – Laurel, Haakon & Ulf

Berserker Babies – the sisters Brenna, Sabine, Muriel, Fleur
and their mates
Night of the Berserkers – the witch Yseult's story
Owned by the Berserkers – Fern, Dagg & Svein
Tamed by the Berserkers – Sorrel, Thorsteinn & Vik
Mastered by the Berserkers – Juliet, Jarl & Fenrir
Surrendered to the Berserkers – Rosalind and her mates

Berserker Warriors
Ægir *(formerly titled The Sea Wolf)*
Siebold with Ines Johnson

ALSO BY LEE SAVINO

For film and TV rights inquiries: <u>lee.savino@leesavino.com</u>

Paranormal romance

Berserker Saga

Sold to the Berserkers

Mated to the Berserkers

Bred by the Berserkers (FREE novella only available at www.leesavino.com)

Taken by the Berserkers

Given to the Berserkers

Claimed by the Berserkers

Rescued by the Berserker

Captured by the Berserkers

Kidnapped by the Berserkers

Bonded to the Berserkers

Berserker Babies

Night of the Berserkers

Owned by the Berserkers

Tamed by the Berserkers

Mastered by the Berserkers

Surrendered to the Berserkers

Midnight Doms with Renee Rose

Alpha's Blood

His Captive Mortal

The Virgin and the Vampire

(All Souls' Night anthology exclusive)

Werewolves of Wallstreet with Renee Rose

Big Bad Boss: Midnight

Big Bad Boss: Moon Mad

Big Bad Boss: Marked

Sci fi romance

Planet of Kings with Tabitha Black

Brutal Mate

Brutal Claim

Brutal Capture

Brutal Beast

Brutal Demon

Tsenturion Warriors with Golden Angel

Alien Captive

Alien Tribute

Alien Abduction

Dragons in Exile with Lili Zander

Dark Mafia Romance

Mafia Brides

Revenge is Sweet

Vengeance is Mine

A Dark Mafia Romance trilogy with Stasia Black

Innocence

Awakening

Queen of the Underworld

Beauty and the Rose trilogy with Stasia Black

Beauty's Beast

Beauty & the Thorns

Beauty & the Rose

Cowboy Romance

Rocky Mountain Mail Order Brides

Rocky Mountain Dawn

Rocky Mountain Bride

Rocky Mountain Rose

Rocky Mountain Romp

Rocky Mountain Rogue

Rocky Mountain Daddy

Rocky Mountain Ride

Possessing Pearl

Wild Whip Ranch with Tristan River

Cowboy's Babygirl

Taming His Wild Girl

ABOUT THE AUTHOR

USA today bestselling author Lee Savino has written over 69 steamy romance novels. Bad boys, mafia men, wolf shifters, and dragon shifters in space—her dominant, alpha-hole heroes will stop at nothing to possess their one true love. Happily-ever-after and book hangover guaranteed!

Connect with Lee Savino in her fabulous Goddess Group: https://www.facebook.com/groups/LeeSavino

ABOUT INES JOHNSON

Lover of fairytales, folklore, and mythology, Ines Johnson spends her days reimagining the stories of old in a modern world. She writes books where damsels cause the distress, princesses wield swords, and moms save the world.

If you liked this wolf romance, then you'll love Ines' Dragons; alpha male shifters, fated mates, and steamy romance with a touch of 80's nostalgia!

Find her at: https://inesjohnson.wordpress.com/

∾

Cover by Acacia at Ever After Designs

❀ Created with Vellum